Amy Alice and the Alchemists

Paul Dowell

Published by Lulu
www.lulu.com

ISBN 978-1-84753-083-7

First published in 2007

This edition published 2007

Copyright 2007 by Paul Dowell

Dedicated to Amy and Jonathan
my inspiration

Alchemist *(al-ke-mist) n.* – A practitioner of alchemy.

Alchemy *(al-kemi) n.* – 1. In medieval Europe, a philosophy and
branch of science that sought to find a
way of turning base metals into gold, a
universal cure and the elixir of life.

2. Any seemingly magical power
or process of transmuting

Chemists and Bullies

Amy Alice had a secret, not just any secret, not just a secret bag of sweets hidden under the bed, or a secret diary no-one could find, or a secret boyfriend no one knew anything about. No, this was a secret so secret that Amy was the only person in the whole wide world who new about it, her parents didn't know, her best friends Lucy P and Lucy T didn't have a clue, even granddad was unaware of what Amy was capable of doing, and granddad should have known because he started the secret.

Amy was the most special girl in the world, no one could do what Amy could do, there wasn't a person in China who could do what Amy could do, there wasn't a child in Brazil who had a secret like Amy's, in fact there wasn't a girl, or a boy, from one end of the world to the other who was as special as Amy.

Amy hadn't always been special, before that fateful day in granddads laboratory when it had started she was just an ordinary nine year old who liked playing with her friends, and loved animals but most of all enjoyed spending time with her granddad.

Amy Alice and the Alchemists

Granddad was a very clever man, Amy couldn't think of anyone she had ever met who was as clever as her granddad. He knew everything about nature and science, he could help Amy with all of her homework whether it was mathematics or geography, he could talk about history or sport, but the subject he loved the most was Chemistry. He was so good at chemistry that he had owned his own chemist shop for years, longer than Amy could remember, and was often locked in his laboratory working on new medicines. Amy had never been in the laboratory, in fact no-one had been allowed to enter, granddad said that it was too dangerous because of all the chemicals and medicines that were in there and he kept the door constantly locked.

The day the secret started was still weeks away and today, being a Sunday, was her favourite day of the week because the shop would be closed and granddad would take her on a walk. Sometimes they went to the beach where they would search the rock pools for crabs hiding in the shallows or starfish stranded by the tide, other times they went to the local wood looking for different types of flowers or listening to the birds singing in the trees. Granddad amazed Amy whenever he took her out, there wasn't a plant that he didn't know the name of, and he could identify all the birds from their songs alone.

Amy had just finished her lunch, which she had wolfed down in a hurry, she carried her empty plate over to the sink where her dad was busy washing the pots and pans. A flop eared rabbit came hopping lazily into the kitchen, Amy picked him up cuddling him close, his fur warm and soft against her cheek.

"Can I go to granddads now?" she asked.

"Take your time," her dad said, "you'll give yourself tummy ache rushing your food like that."

"Please. I've finished my lunch."

"What's the rush," he said smiling, "He'll still be there, he won't leave you."

Chemists and Bullies

"But he said he was going to take me somewhere I've never been before, I can't wait to find out where it is. Please can I go now?"

"Go on then, but be careful, straight to the shop and don't talk to any strangers. You know the rules." he cautioned her lovingly.

"Put your coat on Amy, it looks cold outside." her mum added as she fed two green budgies perched on top of the fridge. The apron tied to her waist had a picture of a whale on the front with a caption below it which read "Save the Whales". Amy grabbed her coat, gave her parents a kiss and ran out into the street.

It wasn't long before she reached the end of the main street and looked ahead, shops lined one side of the wide road with a large well planted flower display opposite and a small children's playground had been erected behind the display. There was the butchers owned by Mr. Fennel and his son, Mr.'s Plumptons pie shop which sold bread and cakes as well as her famous pies, a newsagent which was open at all hours, and the local post office which was owned by that nosy Mrs. Pastor, who new everyone's business and would stand gossiping behind the counter for hours to anyone who would listen. Amy's favourite shop, apart from granddads of course, sat right in the middle of the high street. Luigi's Ice Cream Emporium sold the most delicious Knickerbocker glories Amy had ever tasted. Each Saturday Amy and her friends would treat themselves to a mountainous ice cream in Luigi's, they would leave the shop feeling slightly sick but very contented.

The chemist shop stood alone at the end of the road facing Amy, it was really an old house but the downstairs rooms had been converted into a shop many years before, and granddad lived in the cosy little flat above.

The two bay windows that looked out onto the street were crammed with bottles and jars of all shapes, sizes and colours, there were lotions and creams for any amount of ailments and conditions and posters with advice for chicken-pox, acne and measles.

Amy Alice and the Alchemists

The big white door stood in the centre of the house, above the door was fixed a small white triangle decorated with dots which granddad had said had been there for many years and he thought it was very decorative so had never taken it down. Attached to the front of the door was a small sign which read:-

Bernard Alice
Pharmacist and Chemist of High Renown
Lotions and Potions for all ailments

Please mind the step

Amy ran along the street humming happily to herself, I wonder where granddad is going to take me today, she thought to herself. She ran past the butchers shop, all the sausages and meat had been sold the day before and now its windows were bare, past the dark windows of the deserted pie shop and almost bumped into a man as he left the newsagents the Sunday papers tucked under his arm. She gave a wave to Luigi as she ran past and was just about to pass the post office when someone stepped out from behind the corner of the shop and stood in front of her, blocking her path.

Oh no she thought, not you, this was the last person in the whole world that she wanted to bump into. This was her worst nightmare, why did he have to show up, why today, a Sunday, her most favourite day of the week. She began to panic, she looked left and right searching for a way past, but the boy moved from side to side preventing her from escaping.

Chemists and Bullies

"What a surprise," he sneered, "fancy meeting you here."

"Leave me alone Kristian, let me past." she looked over his shoulder to granddads shop, willing granddad to look out of the window and come to save her.

"Not until you give me your sweets and all of your money," he demanded.

"No I won't," she yelled, "my granddad lives there and he's coming out now." she pointed over to the shop.

Kristian looked nervously behind him and, seeing a deserted street, laughed at Amy. He grabbed her coat roughly, tightening it against her throat making her choke before pushing her against the wall bumping her head painfully against the brickwork.

"This is your last chance Alice, give me your sweets or else!"

Amy ran, the back of her head throbbing, her only escape route was back the way she had come. She sprinted as fast as she could hoping to outrun the skinny boy who had been bullying her for months. Kristian gave chase, his curly ginger hair bouncing on his head as he ran. Amy could hear him getting closer and closer and quickly changed direction just as Kristian tried to grab the collar of her coat.

She crossed the road, passing the brightly coloured flowers she headed for the park opposite the row of shops. Running past the slide she looked back, the boy was right behind her a huge grin on his face.

"You can't get away," he shouted, "just give me your money."

Amy was exhausted, she stopped and started to cry, what's the point she thought, I'll never get away from him. She looked up at the sky and sighed, I wish someone would make him stop.

She looked at him tearfully, "Please leave me alone. Why do you keep doing this?"

Kristian walked up to her, he wasn't much taller than her and he leaned in close so his pale face with his little freckled, piggy nose was inches from hers.

"Because I can," he sneered and pushed her to the ground.

Amy Alice and the Alchemists

Amy hit the grass with a painful bump and tears welled up in her eyes.

"I'm sorry." he said, "Did that hurt, here let me help you up." he went to help her to her feet but Amy ignored his offered hand.

She slowly got up to face her tormentor, as soon as she was standing he again shoved her to the ground laughing cruelly.

"Who's going to stop me?" he taunted, "Not your little girly friends, not if they know what's good for them. Right, give me your sweets and all your money. Now!" he demanded.

Amy started to cry softly as she rummaged in her coat pocket and handed over a small bag of sweets and the money her father had given her that morning.

"Thanks very much," he gloated as he grabbed them from her hand, "It would have been much easier if you had handed it over straight away, wouldn't it? I hope you won't be as silly next time or I might have to hurt you again, understand?"

Amy watched him walking away laughing and slowly stood up. She brushed herself down and followed him out of the park watching him eat the sweets she had been saving for her afternoon with granddad. She made sure she kept her distance, waiting until he disappeared out of sight before walking dejectedly up to granddads shop. She knew that she should tell someone about him but he had warned her that if she did he would get her again and make it even worse. She would just have to try and avoid him as much as she could.

Amy knocked on the door of the shop and waited, it only took a few minutes before she could hear granddad moving about inside. Several bolts could be heard being unfastened and then Amy heard the key turning in the lock before the door was opened and granddad stood before her.

"Ahh, my little princess, in you come." he opened the door wider and stepped aside to allow her to enter. "Now then what's wrong, has something happened?" granddad could tell that Amy was upset.

Chemists and Bullies

"No I'm alright," she answered trying to put a smile on her face.

"Are you sure? I can always tell when there's something wrong, and you don't look very happy at all."

"I'm ok granddad, where are we going today?" she asked, quickly trying to change the subject.

He peered at her carefully over the tops of his silver framed spectacles before replying, "I thought that we could go to farmer Ducks farm and watch him feeding the lambs."

Amy cheered up straight away, a big beaming smile spread across her face and she forgot about the pain in her back and the bump on her head.

"That would be great, but will it be ok."

"Yes, I've already checked with farmer Duck and he says it will be fine. I just need to get my coat and then we can go."

They walked through the shop, it was a very old shop and hadn't changed since the time granddad first bought it many years ago, a smell of cough medicine and disinfectant filled the air. Against the walls to the left and right stood racks with all kinds of bandages and plasters, creams, lotions, cough sweets and tonics.

A long counter faced the door, on the counter stood a very old looking till with big round keys that, when pressed, caused a price tag to shoot up out of the top of the machine informing the customer of the amount to be paid.

Behind the counter the wall was covered with shelves from the floor up to the ceiling, right in the very centre of the shelves was a set of scales granddad had owned for years, small metal discs of varying sizes were piled neatly on either side. The other shelves were littered with bottles and boxes of medicines and tablets for any illness or condition you could think of.

They made their way through a gap in the counter and through a door in the back wall which lead to the staircase and the back door, granddads coat hung on a hook at the bottom of the stairs, he put on his coat and after locking the front door they made their way over to the farm.

Amy Alice and the Alchemists

Amy was happy again, she always was when she was with her granddad, what had happened earlier was forgotten, Kristian had disappeared from her mind and she laughed as she watched the lambs being fed. Before long it was time to go, they set off on their way home.

"Was everything alright today? You seemed a little upset when you arrived this afternoon."

The images of Kristian came flooding back into her head. She considered telling granddad about him. Would it be worth it, she thought, what could he do, it would probably only make things worse.

"No, I'm fine granddad, honest." she lied smiling weakly.

"Well, if there's ever anything you need help with you only have to ask you know."

"I know, thanks."

Amy changed the subject to the farm and the lambs, they continued their journey home on a much happier note and Amy pushed the thoughts of Kristian far out of her head. Until it was time to go back to school that is!

That week Kristian was at his worst, he stole her sweets twice, he pushed her over into a dirty puddle covering her smart red uniform with muddy water. He pulled her hair, nipped her, called her names and put a big black spider into her pencil case making her scream with shock when she went to get a pencil to start her work.

Amy's school life was becoming more and more miserable. When she told her teachers about Kristian they didn't believe her because he was always so well behaved in class. The teachers thought she was exaggerating, Kristian always made sure there was no one around when he picked on her or called her names, or he would chase after her on the way home from school to torment and tease her.

Not one of the teachers had ever spotted him doing anything remotely wrong and wouldn't listen to Amy. She just couldn't think of how she was going to stop him or who would help her, she sat and daydreamed about weekends when she would be with granddad, happy and carefree without any worries and where Kristian couldn't get her.

Shadows in the Dark

The chemist slept soundly in his bed, he hadn't been feeling too well so he had taken some of his tonic, which was very good for colds and coughs and was also excellent at keeping the slugs off his cabbages, and he had gone to bed early. It hadn't taken him long before he had fallen into a deep sleep and as the evening turned to night and the dusky sky became darker the sound of traffic from outside gradually dwindled away. It was now deep into the early hours of the morning, the church bells rang twice, although no one would hear them, and then fell silent. The chemist slept deeply, all that could be heard was the gentle rhythmic sound of his breathing.

Outside, the street was deserted, the dim lights from the street lamps cast deep shadows. From along the street two figures crept closer and closer towards the chemist shop, they hadn't used the van because the sound of the engine may have woken someone up, and they didn't want to be seen. They moved silently from one shadow to the next, their dark clothes blending in with the darkness making them almost invisible. Crouching down behind a car they listened for any sounds and, hearing nothing, they crept to the dark recess of a nearby shop doorway.

Amy Alice and the Alchemists

They paused briefly as they scanned the chemist shop, the lights were out and the curtains upstairs were drawn. They looked at each other through the narrow slits of their balaclavas and nodded. Crouching down low they scurried across the road and hid behind the corner of the chemist shop. One of the pair moved forward and took a small bundle of tools from the pocket of his dark jacket. The tools resembled thin keys and he went to work on the lock of the shop door, he inserted one of the tools into the lock and twisted and turned it but the lock remained fast.

He tried each tool in turn, taking his time, making sure he didn't make a sound. Eventually he heard a small "click" and nodded to his partner. He gently pushed open the door and he reached inside to grab the bells hanging above the entrance and stop them from ringing out.

They stepped into the shop and closed the door silently behind them. Looking around the dark interior of the shop they could see the silhouettes of shelves and racks dotted around, as their eyes became adjusted to the dim light they made out the counter and doorway beyond. They made their way across the shop floor, avoiding contact with any objects in their way and passed through the gap in the counter. The door to the stairs stood before them, they paused yet again listening, straining to hear any sounds of movement from upstairs. The building remained eerily silent and one after the other the intruders tiptoed up the narrow staircase. They took each step at a time, gently placing one foot onto a stair and with gritted teeth waited for it to creak or groan under their weight. The old wooden stairs kept quiet and they slowly made their way to the top.

On the landing at the top of the stairs they were faced with three doors, they stood stock still, without thinking they held their breath trying to pick up the smallest sound which would tell them which room the chemist was sleeping in.

The old man lay in his bed, the tonic he had taken earlier had sent him into a deep sleep and he had drifted from one dream to the next unaware of the strangers who now stood outside his bedroom door. He muttered in his sleep, rolled over onto his back and started to snore softly.

Shadows in the Dark

The door to his bedroom slowly opened and the two dark shadows of the intruders invaded the small room. The first of the pair crept round to the far side of the bed, he unzipped his jacket and reached up to take something from around his neck.

As he lifted his hands away he held a long golden chain, on the end of the chain hung a small crystal. Even in the dim light of the bedroom the crystal glinted, the shiny blue gemstone spun slowly on the end of the chain and the room seemed to become lighter as the dark figure of the stranger held it out.

One black clad arm reached out and gently shook the chemist, the old man muttered and turned over, again the arm gently shook him and this time the intruder started to talk to the chemist.

"You are going to wake up," the stranger intoned in a soothing whisper, "when you wake you will not be frightened."

Again the chemist muttered, his eyelids fluttered but remained closed and then he settled back into a peaceful sleep.

"When I tell you to wake up you will do as I say, you will not be frightened, we are your friends." While he spoke he held out the crystal in front of the chemists face. "Wake up!" he whispered in a calm, soft voice his mouth close to the sleeping mans ear.

The chemist's eyes opened slowly, instantly they were drawn to the crystal which spun in front of his face. He seemed entranced by the blue stone which turned one way then without slowing changed direction and spun the other way.

"You will get out of bed now," the voice ordered gently.

The chemist pulled back the bed covers and swung his spindly, pyjama clad legs out of bed, all the time keeping his eyes fixed to the magical crystal.

"Stand up" he stood up, his eyes were wide as he watched the gemstone appear to dance before him. "You like the stone don't you?"

"Yes," he answered in a far away voice.

Amy Alice and the Alchemists

"If you follow me you will have it, because I am your friend. Will you come with me?" the voice pleaded mockingly.

"Yes, you are my friend" he mumbled slowly as he followed the mysterious figure out of the bedroom and down the stairs.

At the bottom of the stairs the second person threw a dark coat over the chemists pyjamas and pulled a hat from his pocket which he put onto the mans head.

They led him across the shop floor and opened the front door, the chemist's eyes never leaving the twinkling crystal. They left the shop and headed back down the street the way they had come, moving from one dark doorway to the next. Three dark, faceless figures, not seen by anyone, not heard by a soul, three black shadows disappearing into the night.

A Secret Meeting

It was Sunday morning again and Amy was looking forward, as she always did, to seeing granddad. She was in the kitchen of her home when the telephone rang and she heard dad answer it. "Hello," a pause, "Ok dad, I'll tell her. Don't you worry, and make sure you look after yourself. See you when you get back. Bye." and he replaced the phone on the hook.

Amy didn't like the sound of that and her worries were confirmed when dad entered the kitchen. Amy looked up at the tall figure of her father, he stood smiling at her, she noticed he was wearing his favourite T- shirt again, the one with the picture of a rhinoceros on the front and a caption that read, "Rhino Rescue, Keep Them Safe."

"That was your granddad on the phone, I'm afraid he has to go away on some urgent business and you won't be able to go round today."

Amy felt really disappointed, "When will he be back?" she asked.

"He said he would just be away for a few days, he'll be back before you know it."

Amy wondered where granddad could have gone, he sometimes went away for one or two days but it was always during the week, he had never gone away on a Sunday before. She sulked around the house all day, this is the most boring Sunday I've ever had she thought to herself. Unfortunately for granddad this was anything but a boring Sunday.

Amy Alice and the Alchemists

The hall was huge, the walls were lined with dark wood panels, empty hooks dotted the walls where the pictures and paintings which had hung there for years had been removed. In their place hung two large tapestries, one on each wall. The first had three archaic looking symbols painted on it, one above the other. The second was decorated with triangles, two pointing upwards and two turned upside down, the latter pair had rough lines drawn through their centre. Large round tables filled the room, in the centre of each table stood a small silver cauldron surrounded by several bottles made from the same shiny metal. On a raised platform in front of the big arched window stood a long table with four high backed chairs. Granddad sat on one of the throne like chairs and surveyed the people who were entering the room.

They entered through large double doors in twos and threes chatting amongst themselves like old friends. Every now and then someone would see a face they recognised and hadn't spoken to for years, hands would be shook vigorously and backs would be slapped. Eventually the chairs around the tables filled up and the doors were closed.

Granddad slowly stood up, the three chairs beside him stood ominously empty.

The chatting and talking around the tables gradually reduced to a whisper as the congregation became aware of his presence.

Granddad wore his silver spectacles and looked very important in his long white robes. The robe was fastened at the neck with a large silver brooch and hung open to reveal a shimmering golden robe beneath. The outer robe was trimmed with the same silky, golden material all round the hems and at the end of each arm. The golden trim was decorated with white silk symbols, there were triangles and circles, crosses and diamonds intermingled with dots and dashes of various sizes.

There were hundreds upon hundreds of people crowded into the great hall, all dressed in white gowns, but not one of them had the same golden trim. The gowns of those sitting at the tables closest to granddad, who all happened to be wearing silver framed spectacles, were trimmed with a deep purple velvet, behind those were younger men, only a handful of these wore glasses, whose gowns were trimmed with a rich red.

A Secret meeting

Around the walls of the room stood young fresh faced men, some of them only boys, who waited patiently to be called upon. These assistants wore the same white gowns, which were trimmed with grey but lacked the archaic symbols which decorated the more colourful trim of their elders.

Once the room fell silent granddad clapped his hands and the large doors opened. All eyes turned to watch the young assistant as he walked down the centre of the aisle carrying a small ancient looking wooden box, on the lid of the box was drawn a circle with a line running through it from side to side. He placed it on the table in front of granddad and took one step back before speaking.

"I bring to you the salt." he moved away to take his place by the panelled wall.

Granddad picked up the box and held it up high, "Behold," he called out in a clear commanding voice, "I give to you the body!"

All eyes turned once more to the door as the second assistant entered. He carried a ceramic vial, a large stopper made from the same ancient pottery protruded from the neck. On the side of the vial a triangle with a cross attached to its base could be seen.

The young man placed it on the table next to the box, took one step back, and said quietly, "I bring you Sulphur," he also moved away and stood by the wall.

"Behold, I give you the soul!" cried granddad as he held out the vial for all to see.

Finally the last of the assistants, who was only a young boy, entered the hall. He strode up the centre of the aisle confidently, carrying a small round, silver bottle. He approached granddad, nodded his head and then placed the bottle on the table before speaking.

"I bring you the Mercury," he said before moving away to stand by the first two boys.

"Behold I give you the spirit!" granddad arranged the three items along the front of the table before speaking once more.

Amy Alice and the Alchemists

"The opening ceremony is now complete and I must press on to more serious and frightening matters. I have called you all here today to pass on some grave news." He took a deep breath before continuing.

"As you are aware two years ago we lost a dear colleague when Ernest Wellbright disappeared mysteriously never to be seen again. And only six months ago we were shocked at the disappearance of Duncan Heatherbridge who went missing from his shop in the middle of the night. As you can see the chairs beside me are now all empty and it is my responsibility to inform you that another Master Alchemist of the Gold Order has disappeared in strange unexplained circumstances."

The audience gasped at the announcement and started to whisper to each other.

"Gentlemen, could I please have your attention," the room became silent again, "Last night Albert Ecclestone, a dear friend, colleague and inspiration to us all, disappeared from his shop in Cottonsworth. He seems to have left his shop freely as no signs of intruders could be found and his shop remains in a clean and tidy condition." granddad paused and looked around at the people before him who sat staring at him, unable to believe what was being said.

"As the last member of the Gold Order and the one remaining council leader, I would like to ask the Society for their views on this tragic event."

On a table near to granddad a tall grey haired man whose robes were trimmed with purple stood up to speak.

"Senior Alchemist Unsworth" granddad bowed to him and sat down, he looked small in his huge chair with its ornate carvings etched into the wooden back and arms.

Unsworth's robes hung open revealing his purple under robe, he took his silver spectacles from his face and held them in his hand. " I am assuming that Master Alchemist Ecclestone's family have informed the police."

A Secret Meeting

"That is correct." answered granddad

"Then I feel that we should remain calm and leave the investigation to them. I do not think we can help with this matter. Any interference from ourselves may hinder the police rather than help them and will also put our secret society at risk of being discovered." Unsworth sat down on his seat.

Granddad stood and again spoke to the worried faces before him, "These are very sensible statements and I am sure that this is probably the correct course of action but if anyone has something to add please speak up." he peered over the top of his glasses waiting for a response.

Towards the back of the room a youngish man wearing red trimmed robes stood to speak. Although not very old the hair at his temples was already tinged with flecks of silver.

"Alchemist Fairfield of the first degree," granddad pointed out as he introduced him before slowly relaxing back into his seat.

"Master Alchemist," he bowed his head before continuing, "when our colleagues disappeared we decided to do as my friend Senior Alchemist Unsworth has suggested and leave the mysteries to the police, and on each occasion nothing has been done. The police can find no trace of those poor men and they seem to have vanished into thin air. I think it is time we took responsibility for our own safety and I think we should find out who is behind these disappearances and what it is they are after." this caused an outbreak of conversations around the table.

Cries of "Outrageous" and "What's he thinking of" were mingled with calls of "Here, here," and "It's about time,"

Again granddad stood and waited for the noise to recede, "I am aware that there are mixed feelings about this and therefore I shall put the decision to a vote. Each table shall vote for, or against, our society investigating the incidents, without the help of the police. The voting will be conducted in the traditional manner."

Amy Alice and the Alchemists

Granddad sat upright, staring over the tops of his glasses, watching each table with great interest. Heated conversations could be heard around the room and granddad concentrated hard trying to work out which way the decision would go. Over the years he had learned to anticipate how the society would vote and he was very rarely wrong. The arguments and discussions carried on for what seemed like hours and granddad had changed his mind several times about how it would end. Just as he relaxed, with his decision finalised, someone at one of the central tables stood up.

All seven of the occupants at the table were dressed in red trimmed robes, the man who had stood picked up one of the small silver bottles from the centre of the table and poured the yellow contents into the cauldron. He then chose another bottle and poured this into the cauldron too, the blue liquid from the second bottle mixed with the yellow fluid, the mixture started to bubble and a faint sliver of smoke rose into the air.

The two liquids swirled around inside the cauldron spinning and turning and the bubbles rose faster and faster, gradually the blue and yellow colours disappeared and in their place was a boiling red substance.

The smoke rising from the silver cauldron grew thicker and thicker and became darker and darker until above the table floated a small dark red cloud. Around the room similar events had taken place, more and more clouds filled the air, some of them were red and others were a bright green. It was impossible to tell which was the dominant colour, as each new cloud appeared the balance would shift to red then green and back to red again.

One table remained without a cloud, this was the table that Unsworth was sat at. The discussion at this table had been the most heated and voices had become raised and angry as the men disagreed over how they should vote. Eventually they came to a decision and one of the purple robed occupants rose to pour the ingredients into the cauldron. The room became quiet, the red and green clouds floating around the room were evenly numbered and the final decision lay on the colour of the cloud that would rise from the small silver pot sat in the centre of the table.

A Secret Meeting

Slowly the concoction started to bubble and swirl and the smoke rising from it grew thicker and thicker until eventually a small bright green cloud floated above their heads. Unsworth slumped in his chair the look of defeat clear to see.

Granddad stood up, his intuition had again been correct and he had guessed the outcome long before the clouds had started to rise.

"The society has voted and the decision is that we shall stand against this unseen enemy. We shall uncover their identity." he paused, his words growing stronger and becoming more powerful as he spoke, "We shall discover their motives," another meaningful pause, "And we shall put a stop to their activities once and for all."

A spontaneous round of applause broke out from several tables. This was quickly taken up by the rest of the audience who were obviously inspired by the words of their most senior member.

From the side of the room a small voice called out above the noise.

"I would like to volunteer and take on the task of discovering who is behind this." The room fell silent immediately and all eyes turned to the young man who was stood at the side of the room. His cheeks flushed with embarrassment when he realised everyone was looking at him but he stood proud with his head held high.

"Master Alchemist Alice it would be a great honour if the society would allow me to take on this task." This was the same young man who had entered the hall at the start of the meeting carrying the box containing the salt.

Granddad thought for a moment before saying, "Jonathan Polldown has volunteered and I am confidant that he is able to carry out this dangerous task, but I must ask the society that if anyone disagrees let them now speak." the room remained quiet.

"Very well." he turned to Jonathan, "You have been very brave to volunteer and the society congratulates you. You are hereby granted permission to root out this evil and deliver their identity to us. Go carefully and return to us safely." Granddad bowed low and turned to the rest of the Alchemists. "It is in your own interests to remain vigilant until this mystery is resolved. Return to your shops and pray that our friends will be found and our futures will be safe."

The alchemists filed from the room muttering quietly amongst themselves. Unwin stood at his table peering at Granddad, a faint, sly smile curling the corners of his mouth. Turning quickly on his heels he made his way out of the room, striding purposefully along the centre aisle, looking down his nose at his fellow alchemists his head held high. As the room emptied granddad slumped in his chair a look of worry etched into his tired face.

Doppelgangers Delight

Another Sunday afternoon and Amy knocked on the door of granddads shop and waited. Granddad must have been waiting behind the door as it flew open seconds later. "Come in, come in!" he said hastily.

Amy had been looking forward to seeing granddad because of the horrible week she had had due to Kristian but granddad seemed even more excited than her as he ushered her through the shop.

"I have a surprise for you today," he smiled, his wide blue eyes shining brightly.

"Where are we going?" Amy asked. Granddad had never been as excited as this about any other outings they had been on and his enthusiasm baffled Amy.

"We aren't going anywhere. Follow me." granddad led Amy through the shop and out into the back garden.

Amy thought about telling granddad about Kristian but decided that she didn't want to spoil their day by mentioning it, anyway granddad would probably say the same as her teachers and accuse her of over exaggerating.

Amy Alice and the Alchemists

The garden was surrounded by an old crumbling wall that towered above their heads, it was covered mainly by a large lawn, an old swing stood in its centre and a weed covered path ran down the side. They followed the path to the bottom of the garden and stopped in front of granddads shed. The shed had stood here between the pear trees for as long as Amy could remember but she had never been allowed in.

She had often daydreamed about what was hidden inside, but when she questioned granddad all he ever told her was that it was just chemists stuff and far to boring for little girls to worry about.

They stood outside the door of the shed and granddad looked down at Amy.

"I am about to let you in on one of the greatest secrets you are ever likely to come across." he paused looking unsure about whether he should tell her more before continuing, "What you see inside must always remain our secret, you cannot tell anyone about it. Do you promise to keep it a secret?"

Amy swallowed what felt like a huge lump in her throat before answering, "Yes, I promise."

Granddad turned to the door and took from his trouser pocket a tiny little glass bottle. He uncorked the bottle and carefully poured a single drop of the contents onto the old rusted padlock which secured the shed door. The tiny silver droplet resembled a caterpillar as it crawled into the padlock disappearing into the keyhole.

Amy had often examined the lock when she had been playing in the garden, it looked to have been unused for years and completely locked solid with rust. The lock now appeared to be changing, the dark brown rust was slowly disappearing until eventually a gleaming new lock had taken its place. The shiny silver lock popped open of its own accord and granddad removed it from the door. Granddad pulled the door open and they both walked into the shed, the little girls eyes opened wide as she surveyed the interior of what she thought was just an ordinary garden shed.

Dopplegangers Delight

The interior of the shed was illuminated by four torches attached to the walls, their flames flickered in the light breeze as the door was opened. The objects standing in the shed looked like they had been here for hundreds of years, Amy felt like she had stepped back in time as she looked around.

In the centre of the room was what looked like an open fireplace with a large stone chimney rising up to the roof. Over the fire hung a large black pot that Amy thought resembled a witch's cauldron and attached to the side of the fireplace was a large set of bellows. Behind the chimney a dirty red curtain was pulled across the room splitting the shed in half.

Around the walls were rickety looking wooden shelves that were occupied by a variety of ceramic jugs and vases each one decorated with symbols that were totally unknown to Amy. On another shelf there were glass bottles and jars, bits of copper and tin and a small roll of a silken fabric. A large bench stood along one wall, on the bench was a mortar and pestle which appeared to be made from some sort of stone, and a magnificent collection of plants or, to be exact, parts of plants. The table was covered with nettle leaves and flower stems, seaweeds and dandelions, various types of bark sat in one corner and a bowl full of roots occupied another. Amongst all the clutter, in a little brown plant pot, stood a lovely yellow daffodil.

"Welcome to the world of Alchemy," granddad said after a short while.

"The world of what?" asked Amy, who was by now feeling a little bit confused.

"Alchemy." repeated granddad slowly. "It is an ancient art and, as far as normal people are concerned, died out many hundreds of years ago. But it never did disappear, it is still here, in every city in the land, in any village across the world. In all the towns from here to Timbuktu you will find an Alchemist."

"But I thought you were just a chemist,"

Amy Alice and the Alchemists

"Every one thinks we are just chemists. You see hundreds of years ago Alchemists were ridiculed because of their beliefs and laughed at because of their outdated ideas about medicines. They were forced from towns and cities until eventually it appeared that they had disappeared for good. But they didn't disappear, they changed their name and became chemists and professed to use more scientific methods which were accepted by the public, but in reality every chemist in the land was using the ancient methods of the Alchemist in secret."

"Does that mean all chemists today are really Alchemists?" Amy was fascinated, she wondered whether granddad was just telling her a story, this couldn't be true, could it? But what about the lock, that had been a pretty amazing trick.

"Yes, in every chemist shop in the world you will find a laboratory like this one. It may be in a spare room or in a cellar, it could be in the attic or even in the garden shed, but it will be there somewhere, locked away from prying eyes, a secret to be kept for ever."

"But if you only make medicines that help people why do you have to keep it a secret?" she was gradually starting to believe that he was telling her the truth.

"An Alchemists main role in life is to help people who are sick, we make medicines and ointments that can cure almost anything. We are constantly experimenting with different recipes trying to find new cures and remedies but sometimes they do not work out as we expected. A lot of the potions we create can have magical affects, such as the "open sesame" potion I used on the padlock. I have known some Alchemists to stumble across potions of invisibility, some have found potions that could make them fly like a bird and others have created potions that gave them super human speed or strength. But the one potion that eludes us all, the only recipe that has baffled Alchemists over the years, the one secret that all Alchemists have worked to uncover for centuries is the ability to turn everyday objects into gold!"

Dopplegangers Delight

"Has no one ever discovered it?" Amy was now totally engrossed in what she was being told.

"It is believed that the ancient Alchemist, Hildegard of Bingen, discovered the secret in about 1142, it was forgotten for many years and then rediscovered by the Alchemist Paracelsus in 1539 but was then lost with him when he died and no one has discovered it since, although many have tried."

"Have you tried granddad?"

"I have been trying most of my life Amy, and I have risen through the ranks to become one of the most accomplished Alchemists in the country, but I need help, and that's were you come in."

"What can I do?"

"All Alchemists have an apprentice to help them search for the secret, but I haven't had an apprentice for several years now, not since Harris left." a cloud of sadness appeared to pass across his face, but then he smiled as he continued. "I want you to become my new apprentice, I want you to learn my secrets and hopefully help me to become the first Alchemist for almost five hundred years to find the secret. Do you think you would like that?"

Amy nodded, unable to answer.

"Good, we might as well start now." granddad showed her to the fire place, "this is called an Athenor, the fire heats up the ingredients in the pot as we mix our potions. The bellows are used to make the fire hotter depending upon which medicine we are making." He pointed to the shelves, "These contain my ingredients such as Mercury, Silver, Copper and Tin. On the table are all the plants we use, we use a lot of plants in our potions and you will eventually know the names and uses of them all, for example this nettle," he held it up seemingly unaffected by the stinging plant, "is known as Urtica Dioica and the leaves are a good source of tin." he placed it back down and picked up a piece of tree bark, "The bark of the red cedar, also known as Juniperus Virginiana, contains Lead, and Fucus Vesiculosus or bladder wrack," the bark was replaced by a piece of dried seaweed, "contains mercury."

Amy Alice and the Alchemists

Amy's head started to swim with all the strange names and facts granddad was throwing at her and it must have shown on her face because he reassured her gently.

"Don't try to remember all of these yet, you will learn them in time."

"What's that?" Amy pointed to a glass bottle which had caught her eye. The contents of the bottle slowly changed colour, turning from blue to orange, then green and purple and red and yellow. It continued to change as Amy watched it, a rainbow of colours contained in one small bottle.

"That's one of my newest discoveries. I call it Doppelgangers Delight."

"Doppel what's delight?" she asked screwing up her nose.

"Doppelgangers Delight." he repeated, "A doppelganger was a mystical creature from old stories. It was told that they were small goblin like creatures that lived in dark caves. They were able to change their shape and take on the appearance of their prey before sneaking up on them and taking them by surprise."

"Does it work?"

Granddad turned to the large bench at his side and lifted up the little brown flower pot Amy had noticed when she first entered the shed. Amy was amazed to see a bright red tulip growing in the pot. She couldn't believe her eyes and her mouth fell open.

"Where's the daffodil?"

"This is the daffodil! I put a drop of the Doppelgangers Delight onto a dandelion plant I had and it just keeps changing. It turned into a rose first, then a poppy, then a lily and this is the second time it's been a tulip. It's been like this for weeks and just keeps changing, but it hasn't died so I think my potion is safe."

"When can I start to make potions?" Amy was now totally engrossed in the new world granddad had opened up to her and she couldn't wait to learn more.

"I think we'll start next week, I haven't had an apprentice for such a long time and I'll have to try and remember the first lessons."

Dopplegangers Delight

Amy was fascinated by the objects in the shed, but her eyes were continually drawn to the little glass bottle that was still changing colour. As she watched it an idea developed inside her head. It was a risky thing to try, it could even be considered to be dangerous but the plant was alright, it appeared to be healthy and granddad had said he thought the potion was safe. This could be Amy's answer, she had been searching for a way to get rid of that horrible bully Kristian and this little potion could be it.

Granddad disappeared behind the curtain, he lifted a huge water filled jar from the top of an old chest placing it carefully on the floor, inside the jar several long black worm like creatures swam to the surface their sleek bodies undulating gracefully.

"What are those?" Amy asked.

"These are leeches," he muttered as he rummaged around inside the old wooden box, "they were used by Alchemists to help treat people in the olden days." he started lifting books from the chest blowing the thick layers of dust from them.

"I'm sure my old lesson books are in here somewhere," he muttered to himself as he emptied the contents out onto the floor.

Granddads head disappeared into the chest as he reached down to the very bottom. Amy realised this was her chance, but a sense of uncertainty crept over her, she stared at the bottle, her heart pounded faster. Was it really safe, she asked herself? Granddad had said he thought it was safe she answered, but still she hesitated unsure if it was the right thing to do. Then all of a sudden a picture of Kristian's face flashed through her head and she could hear his mocking laughter as he looked down at her sprawled on the floor. This spurred her into action and without thinking she reached for the bottle, she quickly removed the cork, took a small mouthful and replaced it back onto the shelf just as granddad turned to speak to her.

Granddad was speaking to Amy but she wasn't listening, she was concentrating on the liquid in her mouth. The potion tasted nice, a sort of a mix between strawberries and chocolate, now it tasted like gingerbread, then it changed to raspberry ice cream. The flavours kept changing from one to the other, all of them Amy's favourites.

"Are you alright?" granddad asked her, "You look miles away."

"Yyes," she stammered, "I was just thinking about the secret of turning things into gold."

"Never mind that just yet, I've found the lesson books and we can start next week. I think we've done enough for today. Remember you must keep it all a secret."

"I promise."

They left the shed, a small drop of open sesame potion and the shiny new lock turned back into the old rusted lock Amy was used to. They made their way back into the flat, Amy felt so guilty about what she had done. Was it safe? She hoped so. Would it work? She would have to wait and find out. Should she tell granddad? No not yet, she would have to face up to that at a later date. She didn't think he would be very happy, it would probably be best if she waited to see what happened before she confessed. For now all she could do was wait, she was already beginning to feel excited at the prospect of teaching Kristian a lesson and wondering what magical effects the potion would have on her.

Purrfect Pets

Amy wasn't sure whether the potion had worked. It had been two weeks since she had taken a sip of the doppelgangers delight and nothing had happened. She didn't feel any different, she hadn't changed, in fact she was still the same blue eyed girl with pig tails in her hair she had always been. Amy was desperate for the potion to work, Kristian had stolen her sweets on two occasions that week alone and she really wanted to teach him a lesson.

Amy's dad had taken her to the local pet superstore to buy a new birdcage for Peter and Pam their pet budgies.

Amy's parents were mad on animals. Apart from the two budgies they also owned a rabbit, a hamster, a cat and a couple of guinea pigs. Their house was used as a home for all types of creatures that were found ill or injured. At that moment their spare room, which was used to keep the smaller of the sick animals, was home to a hedgehog that had been in a nasty accident with a lawnmower and was lucky to be alive, a noisy duck with a broken wing, three frogs, two toads and a ferret who, shortly after arriving, gave birth to four furry white babies. Outside in the back garden Amy's dad had built two large pens currently occupied by a baby fox that had been found abandoned and a blind crow.

Amy Alice and the Alchemists

Walking through the doors of the store made Amy feel excited, she loved the place and took every opportunity of coming here whenever she could. Purrfect Pets Superstore was huge, there were rows and rows of shelves that seemed to rise right up to the ceiling. On the shelves was everything imaginable for looking after animals, there was dog food, cat food, fish food and budgie seed, cages and beds, blankets and leashes, toys, books and of course pets. In fact anything you wanted for your pet could be bought here and, along with granddads shop, it was one of Amy's most favourite places. Amy headed straight for the animals.

In the very centre of the shop was a large pen containing what seemed like hundreds of rabbits and guinea pigs, around the pen ran a circle of cages, inside the cages were smaller animals. Hamsters and mice ran around plastic wheels, budgies and canaries chirped constantly, chinchillas slept soundly, chipmunks and gerbils bounded about tirelessly, a parrot squawked loudly and amongst them all millions and millions of fish swam in silence. Amy loved them all, she loved the noise and the smell, she walked around with a beaming smile on her face until she reached the cage holding the rats.

She recoiled away from the glass fronted tank as she caught sight of the beady little pink eyes staring at her, the rat twitched its nose, glaring at her, its eyes piercing. It quickly became bored with Amy and started to clean its face with its paws which looked like tiny pink hands. Once satisfied it scurried away to find it's partner hiding in a half gnawed tube, it's scaly tail the last thing Amy saw before it disappeared from sight. A cold shiver ran down Amy's back and she left the pair of rodents to join her father.

Although an avid animal lover Amy had always had a fear of rats and couldn't even stand the sight of them, their beady little eyes and scaly tails had always given her the shivers, she couldn't understand why anyone would want to keep them as pets.

Purrfect Pets

They walked along the aisles and dad read the signs as they passed,
"Fish tanks, hamster cages, chinchilla pens, bird cages. Bird cages! This is
it, this way."

He led Amy down the aisle which was packed from floor to ceiling
with cages of all shapes and sizes. They stopped and looked up and down
the aisle, dad scratched his head, confused by the sheer choice before him.

"That one!" he said after a while pointing up at a cage high above
their heads, "I'll go and find an assistant to help us get it down, you wait
here."

Amy watched her dad disappear around the corner, the cage he
wanted was high above her head on the top shelf. Looking up at the cage
she wondered what it must be like to be really tall, the tallest girl in the
world, a giant even.

As she day dreamed Amy felt different, a tingling sensation started
deep inside her tummy, it grew and grew and started to spread outwards to
her arms and legs until she could feel it right at the tips of her fingers and
toes. It was a strange sensation almost like having pins and needles all over,
her hands and feet felt like they were being stretched and would burst at any
moment. Her face became itchy and when she scratched her chin she felt a
thick, bushy beard where, just seconds ago, there had been smooth pale
skin. She looked at her hands, her fingers were enormous and they too were
covered in short, dark curly hair.

A dizzy sensation came over her, the same feeling she had felt when
she was at the fair and had been stranded with dad at the very top of the
Ferris wheel. Amy looked down, her feet seemed miles away, her white
trainers had been replaced by scruffy brown sandals which exposed her
hairy feet.

Hairy feet!

What was going on?

She started to panic, what if someone saw her, please let me down she
thought.

31

Amy Alice and the Alchemists

As quickly as she had gone up she started to come back down, but not before she remembered to grab the birdcage. The hair on her face, hands and feet disappeared, the tingling in her hands and feet worked its way back along her limbs and faded away deep in her tummy. Faded away but didn't disappear altogether, Amy could still sense it hiding inside her waiting to be called.

What a weird feeling she thought, I've never had a daydream as vivid as that before.

She blinked.

She shook her head.

It couldn't be real, could it?

It must have been real because now she realised she was standing holding the birdcage that, up until a few seconds ago, was perched high on a shelf out of reach to anyone who didn't have a ladder.

Did this mean the potion worked she asked herself, did this mean she was now a doppelganger, did this mean she was now able to deal with that creep Kristian. A mischievous smile formed on Amy's lips just as dad reappeared followed by a store assistant carrying a long ladder.

"Oh, you've got it!" he looked confused.

Amy paused, "Yeah, another assistant helped me," she answered quickly.

Mr. Alice turned to the lady who had followed him and apologised, "I'm sorry to have bothered you but I'm afraid we don't need your help, thank you anyway."

"No problem, always happy to help," she smiled widely showing gleaming white teeth, Amy got the impression that it wasn't too sincere, and the assistant left, struggling under the weight of the ladder.

Mr. Alice looked at Amy, he peered up at the shelf the cage had been stood on, and back at Amy, he shook his head frowning. "Come on we'll go and pay for this." he took the cage from her, it was almost as big as she was, and headed for the checkout.

Purrfect Pets

Amy smiled to herself all the way home. Kristian was in for a big shock, she would practice her new found ability until she was sure she knew how to use it properly and then she would put her plan into action. Granddad would be furious with her of course, she shouldn't have taken the potion, it would probably be best to keep it a secret for now until she could think of a way to tell him without making him too angry.

The smile on Amy's face was soon wiped away when they arrived home, mum was talking with someone as they entered the house and when she saw who it was she felt about as unhappy as she had ever felt.

Sat in the living room chatting away happily with Amy's mum was great uncle Percy. When Amy entered the room Percy wrinkled his nose as if he had encountered a really bad smell. He was from Amy's mother's side of the family and he too loved animals, although he detested children. Percy had never married, Amy's mum had once told her that he had courted her grandmother but she had left him and ended up marrying her granddad. Percy had resented this and never forgiven Bernard and, to this day he hated Bernard with a passion. At this moment he was petting Presley, his grizzled pet mongrel. Presley started to growl at Amy.

"There, there Presley, did the nasty girl scare you, never mind," Percy wiped the dogs great drooping jowls with a stained handkerchief he kept in his pocket. If ever there was a case of dogs looking like their owners then this was it.

Percy was a thin wiry man with great unruly eyebrows that sprouted hair in all directions and a moustache to match. He also had hair protruding profusely from his nostrils and ears, his appearance, and his habits, disgusted Amy.

Presley was a large old dog its course brown hair was dirty and unkempt and he too had an abundance of hair around his muzzle. The grey fuzz around its mouth looked like an untidy beard and his drooping eyes were topped with matching grey bushy eyebrows.

"Say hello to your great uncle Percy," prompted Amy's mum.

"Hello," she said quietly looking at the floor.

Amy Alice and the Alchemists

Percy sneered, his lips curling to reveal yellow stained teeth, and the most disgusting smelly breath Amy had ever come across (your breath would smell too if you ate dog food she thought).

Amy's dad carried the cage into the kitchen before returning to greet Percy.

"Hello there Percy, how are you?" Amy noticed he didn't get too close, he was either afraid of Presley or, more probably, aware of the smell issuing from them.

"I'm fine thank you. When do you leave?"

"In two weeks time." Dad answered, his eyes lighting up at the thought of their forthcoming excursion.

"We'll be glad to watch the house for you while you're away, won't we Presley?" the dog looked at him with its great watery eyes, a huge droplet of drool dangled from its jaws which Percy wiped away with his handkerchief.

Oh no thought Amy, she had forgotten about her parent's trip. Every year they would embark on a crusade to help some poor endangered animals. On one occasion it was to help start a home for orphaned Orang-Utans in Borneo, another year they had helped some Pandas back into the mountains of China and this year they were off to Africa to help move Elizabeth, a three legged Rhino, and her baby into a nature reserve before she became a victim of the poachers.

While her parents were away Percy would be staying, as he normally did, to look after the animals. Amy prayed silently that she would be able to stay at granddads. A couple of years ago granddad had been away for a day at the same time as her parents and she had had to stay with Percy and Presley overnight.

It had been the worst time of her life, Percy didn't speak to her, he gave her notes with instructions scrawled on them when he wanted her to do anything. He made her sleep on the floor so Presley could sleep comfortably in her bed. She was made to clean out the animal cages with her bare hands and the meals were the most disgusting things she had ever eaten.

Purrfect Pets

For breakfast she was served with what she thought was cereal but turned out to be budgie seed mixed with hamster food. At the time they had been looking after a sick mole and when it came to lunch time Amy was faced with worms on toast. She did get chips for tea but unfortunately they had a great dollop of dog food slopped on top. Amy hadn't eaten a thing all day, the food was disgusting but the most revolting sight was watching Percy gobble it all up greedily. She hadn't slept a wink all night either, tossing and turning on the cold kitchen floor while her tummy rumbled madly.

When her parents returned she had tried to tell them what had happened but they thought she was making it up and blamed her vivid imagination. So Amy found herself praying she wouldn't need to stay with Percy and Presley but could spend her time at granddads.

"Will Amy be staying?" Percy asked slyly.

"No she'll be stopping at Bernard's." Amy's mum replied.

Amy sighed with relief.

"Good. I mean, I'm sure she'll have a good time." Percy smiled but to Amy it looked more like a grimace. Percy sneezed, he took the stained, drool covered handkerchief from his pocket and wiped his nose.

Amy felt sick with revulsion at the sight of the dirty, smelly man and his equally disgusting dog that had just broken wind and filled the room with a rather pungent odour. Was she the only one who could tell that he despised her, or was it her imagination. Her parents seemed oblivious to the evil looks he gave her or the hatred in his voice. Eventually they left and Amy felt a lot more relaxed as she watched them waddle away down the street.

In two weeks time her parents were off to Africa and she would be able to spend all day every day with granddad learning about Alchemy, she couldn't wait. Hold on, in two weeks time it would be the start of the summer holidays and school would be closed. Her little plan for dealing with Kristian would have to be put into practice pretty soon or she may not get the chance.

Amy Alice and the Alchemists

Amy made an excuse and disappeared to her bedroom to practice her new found powers. The thought of being able to change into anything she dreamed of was amazing, when she had been in the store she had imagined what it must be like to be a giant and before she knew what was happening she had become one. She wondered what else she would be able to become, this would be fun she thought, the excitement built up inside her until she could hardly contain herself. Not only was she about to have the best summer holidays ever with her granddad but she was also going to teach a nasty little bully a lesson he would never forget.

School Days

Amy learned to control her powers and maintained her secret from everyone. Every now and then she would try them out, just to make sure they were still there, just to check they hadn't faded away. She usually changed while she was in her bedroom and her parents were busy.

Amy's parents were always busy, it was only a few weeks before they left to go to Africa and they were constantly studying maps and flight times, checking their tents and sleeping bags over and over again, and making sure that they hadn't forgotten a thing. They had had a photograph of Elizabeth the rhino printed onto a T-shirt and both her mum and dad constantly wore one of the garments which Amy found highly embarrassing.

This gave Amy plenty of time to try out different things she could change into, she could now control her changing so much that she could change into something and back again before you could blink.

She practiced and practiced her shape changing powers, she wanted to make sure that she would be able to scare Kristian so much that he would stop picking on her for good.

Amy Alice and the Alchemists

Hopefully no one would believe him if he decided to tell anyone that she could change her shape, I mean who would believe it, it was a bit fantastic after all. It would be a bit of a gamble but it was one she was prepared to take. It was the last week of school before the summer holidays and Amy had decided that this would be the week when she would put her plans into action.

Ropeworthy Primary School was an old school, and had been in the village for over a hundred years, it was quite run down and always needed repairs here or there. The school had five small classrooms, an assembly hall, and the dining hall. Outside there was a small playing field which you weren't allowed to play on, especially in the rain because the headmaster didn't like mud being tramped through his nice clean school, and the play yard. The yard ran all the way around the school and had lots of little nooks and crannies which made good places to hide.

It was Monday morning and Amy looked very smart in her red uniform. She was a tall girl, the tallest in her class, with blue eyes and blond hair down to her shoulders. Each day her mum would use a different coloured ribbon to tie her hair into bunches, she never went to school without her hair looking its best and was very proud of her long golden locks. Her two best friends were Lucy Pearson and Lucy Thompson, who every one at school new as Lucy P and Lucy T.

They sat beside each other in the classroom, they played together in the school yard, they had lunch together in the dinner hall and they even walked home together after school. All three of the girls would enjoy playing games, singing songs, chasing each other or telling each other secrets, giggling at what they had been told. Sometimes they would fall out over little things, like all friends do, but it would be quickly forgotten and they would be back to being friends again, the reasons for their arguments forgotten.

It was playtime again and they were playing as usual when Lucy T started to whisper in Lucy P's ear, they both giggled.

School Days

"What are you laughing at?" asked Amy.

"It's a secret." laughed Lucy T. She whispered something else in the other Lucy's ear and again they both giggled.

"Tell me," pleaded Amy she didn't like it when they whispered things about her.

Both girls chorused together, "Amy's frightened of spiders, Amy's frightened of spiders."

"I'm not!" shouted Amy

"I bet you're even frightened of worms." jeered Lucy T.

"No I'm not." cried Amy and she ran off around the corner leaving her two friends laughing behind her.

She hid around the corner and sulked. They were supposed to be her friends, she didn't like it when they made fun of her. They said she was afraid of spiders and worms, she would show them who was afraid of spiders. She looked around the yard, it was deserted, good this was a nice quiet spot where no one could see her.

Quickly Amy changed. She started to shrink. From her sides grew four extra legs, and long black hair started to sprout out all over her body as she grew smaller and smaller.

The two Lucy's were sat on the floor where Amy had left them still whispering to each other and giggling. They didn't see the large black hairy spider come crawling around the corner. The spider was huge, about as big as the girl's heads, it had two big round red eyes and eight long fat hairy legs. At the end of every leg was a little red shoe and each one had a shiny silver buckle.

The spider crawled over to Lucy T, it placed one of its hairy legs onto Lucy's foot, she didn't feel a thing. Slowly the spider crawled up Lucy's leg. As she was sitting whispering with Lucy P, Lucy T thought she could feel something on her leg, a gentle stroking, sort of tickling feeling that itched just a little. She reached down to scratch her leg and her hand fell on something big and hairy.

Amy Alice and the Alchemists

Slowly she looked down and screamed louder than she'd ever screamed before. The spider grinned at her with it's big red mouth. The two girls jumped to their feet and started hopping and stamping on the floor. Lucy P joined in the screaming. The spider scuttled off quickly around the corner, a faint giggly sort of hissy sound coming from it.

One of the teachers came running over to see what all the noise was about, "What's going on," he demanded.

"A spider, a spider," cried Lucy T.

"Is that all" the teacher wasn't impressed, " all this noise over a little spider, come on calm down, this really is a bit dramatic."

"But it was huge, all black and hairy," Lucy T started to cry, the other Lucy joined in, "it crawled on my leg." she added.

Amy appeared from around the corner, "What's wrong?" she asked innocently.

" Did you see the spider?" Lucy P asked.

"That little thing, yeah it went into a crack in the wall," Amy pointed around the corner.

"Weren't you scared?"

"No, like I told you I'm not scared of spiders." and Amy strolled past them with her head up and a sneaky grin on her face.

The teacher shook his head, " Right, back into class, break times over."

Amy hadn't planned on doing that but she was pleased with the way it had turned out, no one had seen her change and no one suspected a thing.

School Days

 The dinner hall was a large room filled with tables and chairs. Along one wall was a long counter which held the meals for that day. The food at school had gradually been getting worse and worse, the gravy contained huge lumps, the vegetables were always soggy and the desserts were disgusting.

As the children entered the hall they picked up a tray and formed a queue at the end of the counter. They would walk along choosing what they wanted from that day's selection and it would be scooped up and slopped down onto their tray by Mrs. Wiggins or Mrs. Trent the two dinner nannies.

Mrs. Wiggins was short and fat, with rosy red cheeks and a mop of shocking red curls on her head. Mrs. Trent was also short and she was even fatter than Mrs. Wiggins, she had great rolls of skin under her chin. She was forever huffing and puffing and constantly dabbed at the beads of sweat on her forehead with the hem of her apron.

That day the meals looked especially revolting, Amy found herself feeling a little playful as she stood in the queue waiting for her food.

"Next!" cried Mrs. Wiggins, as she served up lumpy mashed potato.

"No potato thank you" said a small boy at the front of the queue. Too late, a large spoonful of potato landed on his tray, he looked down at it and grimaced, he was still looking at it when Mrs. Trent covered it in the lumpiest gravy he had ever seen.

"Next," shouted Mrs. Wiggins again.

Amy disappeared behind a large trolley containing knives and forks which was behind the two dinner nannies. She quickly changed into something else. Her skin became bright green and shiny, her feet grew large and flat with webs between her toes. She started to get smaller and smaller and her eyes became bigger and bigger, suddenly a monstrous tongue shot out of her mouth and she swallowed a passing fly.

"Aaaagghh," she gagged.

From behind the trolley a massive green frog appeared, it hopped along the back of the counter behind the sweating dinner nannies until it reached a vat of custard, without pausing it leapt into the sticky yellow liquid.

"A frog!" one of the children in the queue screamed and pointed at the vat.

The two dinner nannies turned and saw the frog swimming around in the custard, what they didn't notice was a gleaming diamond crown sat on the frogs head.

Mrs. Wiggins picked up a large ladle, she smashed it down onto the Amy-frog, but the slimy amphibian was too quick and easily avoided the blow. Mrs. Trent joined in and with a large wooden spoon she too tried to hit the frog. The custard flew everywhere, it was up the walls, on the floors, the counter was covered, the children watching were covered and the two dinner nannies were totally plastered with thick yellow custard. Some of the children started to scream but the screams quickly changed to howls of laughter as they watched the two yellow figures swiping out at anything that moved.

The Amy-frog swam around and around the vat, it swam on its front, it swam on its back, at one point it even climbed up onto the edge of the tub and did a perfect swallow dive disappearing deep into the custard. Blinded by the thick lumpy custard the two fat ladies lashed out completely missing the frog each time.

Tired of its little game the Amy-frog hopped out of the vat and quickly disappeared behind the trolley. Every one was too busy laughing at Mrs. Wiggins and Mrs. Trent to notice Amy join the end of the queue as she quickly wiped the last remnants of custard from the end of her nose.

Suddenly Mr. Graham, the headmaster, entered the hall.

"What's going on," he thundered. Everyone fell silent.

"There was a frog," stammered Mrs. Trent, pointing at the custard.

"A frog" shouted Mr. Graham, his bushy eyebrows quivered, "Who is behind this?" he glowered at the children who all stood with their heads lowered. "When I get to the bottom of this the culprit will be in detention for a month."

He strode over to the end of the counter, his long legs covering the short distance quickly, and picked up a telephone.

School Days

"Mrs. Plumpton, this is Mr. Graham, I have 150 hungry children here and I need to feed them as quick as I can." he paused as he listened, "very good I shall see you soon, thank you." he put down the telephone and turned to face everyone.

"Everybody sit down," they all sat, "you will have something to eat shortly, but I demand that you sit here and wait. Quietly!" he turned to the two yellow dinner nannies "and you two can get this mess cleaned up." and with that he strode out of the dinner hall.

A short time later a small red van entered the school grounds and parked outside the dinner hall, on the side of the van in large white letters were the words:-

Mrs. Plumpton's Pie Shoppe
Homemade Sweet and Savoury Pies

10 Vicars Lane, Ropeworthy.

Tel 5344425.

Out of the van jumped a tall slim lady wearing a long white coat, she walked to the rear of the van and opened the double doors. From inside she lifted a pile of red plastic trays, each one laden with pies. Carefully she carried them inside and laid them down on the counter. She repeated this three times, each time carrying tray upon tray of pies of all different types. There were mince pies, steak pies, and chicken pies, there were pies filled with apples, some with cherries and even some with bananas.

Mrs. Wiggins and Mrs. Trent served up the delicious pies, they were still covered in custard and they glared accusingly at everyone as they collected their freshly baked delicacies. The children didn't dare look at the two ladies, one glance and they would burst into laughter which would only make the angry dinner nannies even more furious.

Amy Alice and the Alchemists

The angrier they got the lumpier the gravy and the sloppier the mashed potato would be tomorrow, but every child in the room thought it was worth it. The children had the best school dinner they had ever had, they were thrilled to have something tasty to eat for a change. Amy was proud of her achievement and she was pleased that her plan had worked, although she wished she could let someone know it had been her who had given them their best school dinner but she knew she couldn't say a thing. No one, apart from granddad, would find out about her secret.

Well Kristian would find out of course, he was the reason Amy had taken the potion in the first place. She couldn't wait to put her plan into action, and because she had had such fun with the two girls and then with the custard she decided tomorrow would be the big day!

The Kristian Incident

K ristian Clapham-Cross was a bully. He wasn't the biggest bully at the school, there were worse bullies than him, but he was a bully all the same. Kristian didn't pick on any of the boys at school, most of them were bigger than him as he was a small, skinny, pale boy with a little turned up, piggy nose covered in freckles, his hair a mass of bright ginger curls. The boys would hit him back if he tried to pick on them. Kristian picked on the little girls who were much smaller than him. Kristian hated girls, and the reason he hated girls was because of his mother.

Doris (pronounced Doreece) Clapham-Cross was Kristian's mother. She, like Kristian and her husband Edward was thin and pale. She had a wicked temper, she would fly into a rage at the slightest thing, especially if she didn't get her own way. She was extremely jealous of her sister Amanda who had married a rich businessman, and vowed that she would live in a big posh house just like her. Because of this the Clapham-Crosses never had much money, all of their money was used to pay for the house that they lived in, they didn't have much left for food or clothes and lived on beans on toast and sardines.

Amy Alice and the Alchemists

They each had one set of special going out clothes, which were always worn when they left the house but were hung safely back in the wardrobe on their return. They would change back into their "house clothes" when they were watching the TV away from prying eyes.

If they were at home in their worn and faded rags and the doorbell rang (to the tune of the national anthem), Doris would rush upstairs, change quickly into her best flowery dress and answer the door with a beaming smile on her face.

The outside of the house was always immaculate, Edward was forever mowing the lawn, painting the fence, or weeding the flowerbeds, under the supervision of Doris of course.

The inside of the house was a different matter, the carpets were threadbare, and the wallpaper was faded and torn. In the living room stood two threadbare armchairs and an old beanbag that Kristian used. The TV was old and only showed programs in black and white pictures. The house was always cold as they couldn't afford to heat it, so they always wore thick jumpers and coats while they watched TV or ate their sardines.

Doris didn't care about the inside of the house, as long as the neighbours thought they were well off she was happy. She even made Edward travel to work in a suit carrying a briefcase and told everyone he worked in a large bank in the city. Edward actually worked as a bin man and would change into his overalls on his way to work.

Edward didn't care though, he had stopped caring a long time ago when he realised that he had a much quieter life by agreeing with Doris' demands. When he didn't agree she would be furious and would shout and scream for hours and hours until she got her own way.

When they were first married they lived quite comfortably in a small terraced cottage, Doris Cross and Ted Clapham became Dorees and Edward Clapham-Cross and they soon moved from 6 Dulling Terrace into The Sanderlings, Acorn Avenue which was a house in the new estate on the edge of town.

The Kristian Incident

Soon they had a little baby boy who they called Kristian, (with a K they would assure people as they peered into the pram). He was a lovely little baby with masses and masses of red curls for hair. Doris would make sure he was always dressed in the best baby clothes you could buy, even if it meant that Edward and she had to go without food for a day or two, it was worth it to see the jealous looks on her neighbours faces.

As Kristian grew up he became more and more aware of his mothers desire to show everyone that they were well off, he hated having to eat sardines all of the time and wished he could receive a brand new toy for Christmas or his birthday instead of a second hand one his mother had bought at the charity shop (she only shopped there to help the people in need she would say). He didn't like the way she shouted and screamed at dad to get her own way and felt sorry for him as he always looked sad and tired.

Kristian began to dislike his mothers actions and vowed he would never allow a girl to treat him like that, in fact he would be the one to be nasty to them, so he began teasing the girls at his school, then he would chase them, he started to pinch and poke them in the classroom, and finally he began to steal their pocket money and sweets.

That day, after Kristian had pinched her sweets for the third time that week, Amy decided it was time to put her plan into action. She waited outside the school gates at home time and when she saw Kristian she began to make fun out of him.

"Curly Shirley, Curly Shirley," she sang, "Hello mop top, is that a birds nest on your head?"

Kristian was furious, he hated people talking about his hair, "I'll get you for that Amy Alice." and he set of chasing her along the road.

Amy ran, she ran up the street and instead of turning left to go home she turned right onto the main road, the road ran through the village and out into the fields that surrounded it. Kristian was gaining on her, shouting threats about what he was about to do to her. Amy had to speed up to make sure he wouldn't catch her yet, she wanted him to catch her but only when they were alone. Amy ran past the fields and headed for Duck's Dene.

Amy Alice and the Alchemists

Duck's Dene was a small wood that ran along the side of the village, it was called Duck's Dene because it, and the fields around it, were owned by farmer Duck.

Farmer Duck was a nice jovial man and he didn't mind people walking in the dene as long as they didn't go trampling in his corn fields.

Amy reached the edge of the dene and glanced back, Kristian was close behind her. She disappeared into the trees and ran along a narrow dirt path. The dene was dark inside, most of the sunlight was blocked out by the ceiling of thick green leaves. The path sloped downwards towards the bottom of the shallow valley that the dean was situated in.

Amy ran as fast as she could, she gasped for breath, her chest heaving in and out. She would have to find a place to hide soon, she was running out of energy and Kristian would catch her, she could hear him close behind shouting at her.

"You wait Amy Alice!" he called angrily, " If you don't stop I'll kill you."

"And if I do stop I suppose you'll leave me alone!" she muttered to herself sarcastically. "Somehow, I don't think so!"

I've got to find a secluded spot she thought, somewhere where I won't be seen.

As she ran she glanced left and right searching for a hiding place. Suddenly a large spotty dog appeared on the path closely followed by a woman holding a long leash. Oh no, thought Amy, this could ruin my plan, I must find a quiet place out of the way.

She darted to the left along an even narrower path that ran through the thick bushes and shrubs, she could hear Kristian close behind crashing his way through the undergrowth.

The path opened out into a small clearing that was dark and quiet. Amy quickly hid behind a bush. Kristian entered the clearing and stopped, he listened carefully, trying to work out where she was hiding. All he could hear were the birds singing and the babbling of a small stream close by.

The Kristian Incident

He tiptoed across the clearing and peered down the path that continued deeper into the trees. Seeing and hearing no sign of his quarry he paced around the dappled centre of the shadowy clearing.

"I know your here." he whispered, "and when I find you you're going to beg me for mercy."

A bush to his left gently rustled and Kristian silently made his way across the clearing, he stopped in front of the large thorny shrub, a beam of sunlight pierced the leaves above illuminating the scene, causing his ginger curls to shine brightly. Listening carefully he could hear her breathing, and shuffling about. He grabbed the bush and pulled it to one side.

"Ah ha!" he cried triumphantly "I've got you now."

Amy wasn't there, in her place crouched a large shaggy, brown bear. Kristian whimpered, the bear stood up on it's hind legs, towering over him. The skinny little boy looked tiny stood in front of the big bear and he backed of quickly, stumbling and falling to the ground. The bear was huge, it had thick shaggy brown fur and long hooked claws. On its head it wore a frilly white bonnet tied in a bow under its chin, a small pair of silver spectacles balanced daintily on the end of its nose.

The bear leaned over the cowering figure of Kristian, its face inches from his, "Who's been pinching my sweets," it growled.

The bear was so close he could smell the porridge on its breath, and see the drool dripping from its mouth. Kristian tried to curl up even smaller, crying and snivelling on the floor.

"If you ever steal my sweets again I'll............" the bear roared, Kristian screamed.

"I'm sorry, I'm sorry" Kristian pleaded "please don't hurt me."

A huge claw came hurtling down towards him and Kristian feared the worst, but the blow never came, instead the bear carefully removed the sweets that were sticking out of the boy's trouser pocket and placed them gently into the pocket of its apron.

Amy Alice and the Alchemists

One huge curved claw slid under the belt around Kristian's waist and he felt himself being lifted up. He flew through the air and landed with a thud in a prickly thorn bush. The bear stomped over and picked the boy up.

Kristian looked like a pin-cushion. There were thorns and needles sticking out all over him. The bear lifted him above her head as if he was as light as a feather and swung him round and round, Kristian started to feel sick, again he found himself flying through the air and this time he landed with a splash in the stream. He felt a big hairy paw grab him by the collar and lift him out of the water.

Holding him at arms length, his feet dangling in mid air, the bear leaned forward close to him and began to speak.

"It makes me quite mad when you keep stealing my sweets. So mad that it makes me want to Eat. You. All. Up" It growled these last words very slowly, licking its lips theatrically.

This had the desired effect on Kristian, he screamed louder than ever. He cried out for help as the bear carried him over to a tree and left him dangling by his jumper on a branch.

"One other thing." it growled, "I don't like you being nasty and cruel to poor animals. You wouldn't like it, would you?"

"I'm sorry," sob, "please leave me alone," sob, "I'm really, really sorry." more gasping sobs.

The bear strode back a few paces, it took the packet of sweets from it's apron pocket. With every word she spoke she threw a sweet at him making him cry out each time one of the hard sweets made contact with his freckled face.

"Don't!"
"Oww!"
"You!"
"Aahh!"
"Ever!"
"Ouch!"

The Kristian Incident

"Pick!"

"Eeehh!"

"On!"

"Ooff!"

"Anyone again!" she screamed the last words as she flung a handful of sweets at the bedraggled sobbing boy.

"Remember, you be a good boy from now on or I'll be back!"

The shaggy bear stomped of crashing through the bushes.

Kristian struggled against the tree unable to free himself from the branch, whimpering and crying pathetically, tears running down his cheeks and his nose running in thick streams down to his chin.

"Are you alright" it was the woman who had been walking her dog, "I heard an awful din and came to find out what it was."

Kristian couldn't answer, huge sobs came from him and his chest heaved in and out, he wiped his nose on the sleeve of his jumper leaving a shiny sticky trail on the red fabric.

"Come on I'll help you down," she loosened his jumper from the branch and the boy slumped to the ground. "My, you're in a bit of a mess aren't you," she looked him up and down. His clothes were torn, he was soaking wet and he had thorns sticking out all over his body. "Who did this to you?"

Kristian didn't answer, he just stood snivelling.

The dog sniffed at him, then trotted over to the nearby bushes it nose close to the ground.

Amy appeared from the bushes and patted the dog. Kristian looked at the ground.

The woman looked from the boy to the girl and back again. Kristian's cheeks glowed red. The woman couldn't believe that this innocent looking girl with blue ribbons in her hair and her school uniform all clean and tidy could have caused so much trouble.

"You mean she....." Kristian ran away crying, Amy and the woman watched him go.

51

Amy Alice and the Alchemists

Amy shrugged her shoulders feigning innocence "Bye," she waved to the woman and strolled along the path eating the last of her sweets.

The woman shook her head, "Sally, come on," she called to her dog and they followed Amy along the path.

On her way home Amy thought about the way things had gone. Hopefully her plan had worked and she would be left alone from now on. She didn't think Kristian would dare tell anyone, he would be too ashamed, no one would believe that a girl could change into a bear, they would think he was mad.

School life was a lot better after the Kristian incident, Lucy P and Lucy T couldn't understand what had happened to him. Every time they saw him he would run away or cross the street to avoid them. Amy said she didn't know why he had changed but thought that maybe the headmaster had found out he was a bully and warned him to stop. They were a lot happier at school knowing they wouldn't be picked on or threatened, and they always kept their sweets.

It was probably time to confess to granddad about what she had done, the potion had done its job and hopefully granddad would be able to create an antidote and return Amy to normal. He would be furious of course, it had been quite dangerous of her to take the potion, anything could have happened. She had to do something about it though, she couldn't go on for ever changing into fantastic creatures, even if it was such fun.

Devious Double

my's parents kissed her goodbye on the step of granddads shop and left for their trip to Africa. Amy waved goodbye as their car headed off down the street, they would be away for four weeks but Amy didn't mind she was used to it, it was the summer holidays and she would have loads of fun staying at granddads and what's more her father had promised he would take her to Disneyland when he got back.

One rainy morning a few days after her parents had left Amy and her granddad were in the laboratory and granddad was showing her how to create what looked to Amy like a medieval torch.

"The Ever Burning Lights Of Trithemius have been used to light the laboratories of Alchemists for thousands of years." his eyes wide with excitement. "The first lesson all new alchemists learn is how to create the ever burning lights."

A jumble of emotions was coursing through Amy as she watched him. She was excited at the prospect of discovering the ancient art of alchemy but was both nervous and frightened at the prospect of confessing about the doppelgangers delight. She had been building herself up to this moment for several days but now that it was here she couldn't bring herself to mention it.

"First of all you take four ounces of Sulphur and a spoonful of calcified Alume."

How could she tell him, how could she explain that she had been so devious to take a potion unaware of its consequences.

"These are put into an earthen Sublimatore, that's a large cauldron, and placed over a coal fire." he hung the pot above the fire, fanned the flames with a couple of blows from the bellows and returned to the table.

She couldn't leave it any longer, the guilty feeling inside her was building and building, a nauseous sensation was tumbling around deep in the pit of her stomach and rising quickly to lodge itself in the back of her throat.

"We then take two and a half ounces of Christallick and add these to the cauldron, remove from the fire immediately and bruise together with a marble pestle."

Granddad was the nicest person she had ever known, and very rarely lost his temper, but she had convinced herself that he would be disappointed to say the least.

"The steaming mixture is poured onto a copper plate and spread thinly, allow to cool for a minute or two and when it has stopped smoking roll into a silk square." he was totally engrossed in his work and failed to notice the pained expression on her pale face.

"This is now placed into a glass tube and when lit will burn for ever." he lit the torch from the flames of another hanging on the wall. The new flame was very small at first but as they watched it grew until a golden yellow flame flickered lazily from the glass tube. Granddad seemed entranced by the new light he had created and gazed at it spellbound.

"I took some of the doppelgangers delight!" she blurted it out.

Granddad kept staring at the flickering light, had he heard her, she wasn't sure, he kept looking at the light for a few more seconds then placed it into a bracket fixed to the wall.

He had his back to her and Amy saw his shoulders slump and his head droop before he turned to face her.

Devious Double

"Why?" he spoke very softly, the disappointment in his face clear to see.

"I wanted to frighten someone" She looked at the floor, too ashamed to make eye contact.

"Who?"

"A boy at school who was bullying me." a tear welled up in her eye and trickled down her cheek.

"You could have come to me for help."

"I know. I am sorry."

"No one needs to put up with bullies Amy, the worst thing you can do is keep it to yourself. You should have told someone."

Amy knew he was right and wished she had told him long ago.

"What's done is done. The important thing is that you must realise that you should never take anything if you don't know what it will do to you, it could have been very dangerous. In fact it might still be so, we don't know what effect it has had on you."

"I feel alright." the sick feeling inside her was starting to abate.

"You may feel alright now but it's the longer term effects that may harm you. What did the potion do to you?"

"You were right granddad, it did make me change. I can change into anything I like just by thinking about it." she was starting to get excited now, thrilled at the opportunity to tell someone about what she could do. "I have changed into a giant, I've been a frog, a spider and a bear."

"You can do this just by thinking about it?" although worried about the effects of the potion he was intrigued by what he was hearing.

"Yes, it's easy."

"And how did you deal with this bully?"

Amy began to tell him about Kristian, about how he had been bullying her for months, calling her names, stealing her sweets and picking on her and how she had dealt with him once and for all.

It was while she was talking that a tiny bell above the door to the lab rang gently.

Amy Alice and the Alchemists

"Some ones at the front door, come on let's see who it is," as he was locking the door to the shed he turned to Amy, "please promise me that you won't ever do anything like this again."

"I promise." she felt awful about it, but at the time she thought it had been her only option, she should have told some one of course, she realised that now. As she hurriedly followed granddad back into the shop she felt confident that he would be able to make her normal again.

The doorbell rang again as they crossed the floor of the shop and granddad opened the front door. The visitor shook out his umbrella, folded it up and left it leaning against the wall in the porch, he then entered the shop as granddad closed the door.

Amy was amazed when the visitor walked into the room. He looked exactly like her granddad, his face looked just like him, he was the same height, he was just as broad as granddad, his greying hair was the same, in fact you couldn't tell them apart. The only difference between the two men was in their eyes. Granddad had large, shiny, blue eyes, happy eyes Amy called them, but the visitor's eyes were narrow and dark and made him look shifty. He was dressed in a smart grey suit with a bright orange tie and the shiniest shoes Amy had ever seen.

"Bernard, it is good to see you, how are you old chap?" the visitor held out a hand.

"I'm alright." Granddad answered shortly, ignoring the offered hand.

"Good, good," the visitor didn't seem bothered at Granddad's rebuff, "and who do we have here?"

"I'm Amy" she answered shyly.

"Ah, you must be Phillip's girl."

"What do you want Samuel?" granddad interrupted.

Amy could tell that her granddad wasn't pleased to see the visitor who's name she now knew.

56

Devious Double

"Bernie, call me Sam, after all I am your brother." he leaned casually against the counter and surveyed the shop, "It's not such a strange thing to do is it? Visiting your brother."

"I would prefer to call you Samuel, if you don't mind, and I would appreciate it if you would call me Bernard!"

"Very well, if you insist," Samuel was unperturbed.

"You're after something, you always are. I never see you unless you want something." Bernard was beginning to lose his patience.

"Ok I'll get to the point. I'm working on something and I need your help."

"I don't think so, I promised that I would never get involved in any of your scams again." Bernard opened the shop door, "I'm too busy to get involved with you and if that's all you have to say would you please leave."

Samuel straightened up, "Too busy are you? What I'm working on would be worth a small fortune for you, and me of course."

"Like I say I'm not interested, too busy."

" I hope whatever it is you are working on is worth it." Samuel walked towards Bernard, "Something interesting is it?"

Bernard glanced quickly towards Amy, "That's none of your business."

Samuel had noticed the look and paused before continuing, "Well if you change your mind give me a call," he reached into his pocket, "my numbers on my card." he offered the card to Bernard who didn't even look at it.

"I don't think that will be necessary." Bernard stood with the front door open "goodbye." he said coldly

"Sorry you feel this way Bernie, I had big plans for us." and with that he picked up his umbrella, opened it out and left.

As he walked down the drive the woman who had been waiting in his large, silver, expensive looking car opened the rear door for him. Once he was inside she closed the door and looked up at the shop before getting back into the drivers seat.

Amy Alice and the Alchemists

The car pulled away from the house and disappeared along the street as Amy and granddad watched from the window. Granddad wondered what could have been so important for his brother to turn up after all these years. He quickly put the thoughts out of his head as he remembered how Samuel had treated him in the past, his brother had always been sly and deceitful and granddad was sure that he hadn't changed.

"I didn't know you had a brother," Amy was a little confused.

"A twin brother to be exact, but I don't see him anymore, in fact I've never seen him since before you were born." granddad sat back into his chair. "We don't get on, never have done really, even when we were young."

"Why?" Amy was now quite interested. "I thought you would be close, especially if you're twins."

Granddad paused, "He's not a very nice person Amy. In fact he can be extremely devious, he's what you might call the black sheep of the family"

"But he looked like he was rich. He didn't look like a troublemaker."

"All the money he has, has been gained by dishonest methods." he stared at the wall remembering some of the things his brother had done before continuing "He calls himself a chemist and a business man but he has made a fortune from other peoples ideas, including mine!"

"A chemist! Just like you?" Amy couldn't believe it, her blue eyes were wide open.

"No, he isn't like me! He steals ideas from other people and claims that they were his." granddad started pacing the floor.

"That's terrible" Amy felt sorry for him as he was now looking quite sad, "What did he take from you?" she asked quietly almost too afraid to ask.

"A lot of things Amy, he has taken from me for as long as I can remember, and the only way to make sure he can't do it is to keep away from him. That's why I don't see him, and that's why I didn't tell you about him," granddad locked the front door and beckoned Amy to follow him upstairs, "I'll tell you about my brother and then you might understand why he isn't to be trusted."

They sat on the sofa with the rain running down the windows and granddad recalled the moments of his life that, up until that time, Amy had never known.

Sibling Rivalry

On the seventeenth of May 1948 Albert and Annie Alice became parents of beautiful twin boys. The twins were born within minutes of each other and they were identical, they both had brown hair, they were the same weight, the same length, they looked the same, they even sounded the same when they cried. The only way you could tell them apart was by looking at their eyes. The first of the twins to be born was named Bernard and he had blue eyes, the second twin was called Samuel and his eyes were a deep brown. Samuel arrived seconds after Bernard as if he didn't want to miss out on anything Bernard may be doing.

Albert and Annie had their hands full looking after the boys, everything had to be done in duplicate. They had to have two of everything, two bottles at meal times, two teddy bears for them to play with, two cots, two prams, whatever baby's needed they had to buy it, twice. Everything had to be done twice too, if one wanted feeding the other would cry to be fed too. If Bernard needed to be changed then Samuel would cry to be changed as well. It was hard work to keep up but the Alice's adored the twins and never complained about how tired they felt.

Amy Alice and the Alchemists

The boys became rivals at an early age. If one twin was playing with something the other would want it, if one of them was being cuddled by mum or dad the other would want a cuddle. Everything seemed to be a competition between them and it took a lot of patience and understanding from Albert and Annie to ensure that one of the twins didn't feel left out or that they started fighting over something.

When they started school it became clear that Bernard was the cleverer of the two. He excelled in nearly all of his lessons, showing a special gift for anything scientific, he learned quickly and always received good reports from his teachers. Samuel, although quite a smart boy, wasn't as clever as Bernard, he was however very good at making friends and became very popular. He seemed to have a way of charming people, including his teachers, and he also received good reports.

On their fifth birthday the boys received a lovely shiny new bike each. Bernard's bike was red and Samuel was given a blue one, but apart from the colour the bikes were identical. They were the same make, the same size and each one had a shiny silver bell on the handlebars. Samuel, however, was jealous of Bernard's bike, he thought that his brother's bike looked a lot better than his and hated watching Bernard ride around the street outside their house or polish the bike every time it got a little dirty. He wanted a red one just like Bernard's instead of the blue one he had been given. Samuel decided that if he couldn't have a red one then neither would Bernard.

One day, not long after their birthday, the boys were playing in the street. Bernard was riding around on his bike and Samuel was sat on the path playing with some toy soldiers. Bernard was going up and down the street trying to make his bike travel as fast as he could, he would stand up out of the saddle and push the peddles with all his might willing the bike to go faster. As he rode past Samuel, for what seemed to Samuel like the five hundredth time, Bernard saw his brother reach behind him and lift up a long stick he had been hiding. Bernard could see the intention in Samuels face but was too close to his brother and travelling too fast to stop or steer away from him.

Sibling Rivalry

As the red bike flashed past him Samuel jammed the stick through the spokes of the front wheel. The stick whizzed around the inside of the wheel and suddenly caught against the forks holding the wheel in place. The front wheel stopped almost immediately but the back wheel kept on turning causing it to lift off the ground and throw Bernard forward over the handlebars and fly through the air screaming. He landed with a thud in the gutter and cried, his head hurt and when he reached up to check the back of his head he felt something sticky. He looked at his hand and cried even louder when he saw it was covered in blood.

"Bernard!" His mother yelled as she ran from the house. "What's happened?" she picked him up and cradled him to her chest, the blood soaking her blouse.

"Samuel did it," the tearful Bernard cried between sobs, "He made me fall off my bike," he pointed to his bike and what he saw made him cry even louder. His bike lay on the floor, the front wheel had bits of wires that used to be spokes sticking out all over, the handle bars were twisted and bent, the saddle had a big chunk missing from it and the lovely red paint on his bike was covered in scrapes and scratches.

"Come on we'll have to get you to the Doctors," mum carried him inside and phoned a friend who arrived in his car and took them to hospital.

Samuel was happy about what he had done and didn't feel guilty about hurting his brother or damaging his bike, he didn't even mind the terrible scolding he received from his father. He was sent to his room and lay on his bed without a care, wondering about how jealous Bernard would be when he saw Samuel playing on his shiny blue bike.

That was the start of the ill feeling between the twins, from then on Bernard didn't trust Samuel, and tried to avoid playing with him whenever he could. Samuel didn't mind, he had plenty of friends and always had someone to play with.

Amy Alice and the Alchemists

As they grew older they drifted further apart, mainly due to Samuels'
devious nature. Bernard couldn't understand why Samuel remained popular
at school, he was always betraying people and telling lies, but his skill at
making people like him always worked to his advantage.

When they were fourteen they had both become members of the
schools science group and would spend one night each week at school
working on electronics, robotics, chemistry or any other projects they were
interested in. Bernard was the star and for the end of term climax he had
been given a special project to present to the group. He worked long and
hard, making sure the presentation would be of the highest standard. On the
evening of the presentation Bernard had everything he needed set out in the
science classroom, he gathered all his beakers and flasks, he had his bunsen
burner and his chemicals, the models he had painstakingly built were dotted
around the classroom, he had his clean white lab coat his mum had carefully
ironed and of course his speech. He was confident he hadn't forgotten
anything. Before he was due to make his presentation he started to feel a
little nervous and, knowing he had plenty of time, left the room to go to the
toilet.

Samuel, who had been hiding along the corridor, saw Bernard leave
and realised this was his chance. I'll show you who's the best in the class,
he thought to himself as he entered the science lab. He quickly lit the
Bunsen burner and placed Bernard's notes over the small blue flame,
watching as the paper curled and floated away in small brown specks.
Almost hypnotised by the flickering paper Samuel realised he must work
quickly and left the burning paper in one of the basins. He poured all of the
chemicals down another basin and coughed as the fumes created started to
fill the room. Bernard's models were thrown to the floor and Samuel
grinned as he stamped on each one, the sounds of his parents praise echoing
in his head. Still grinning Samuel surveyed his damage, that should show
him, he thought and quickly he left the classroom.

Just as Samuel turned the corner and disappeared out of sight Bernard
entered the corridor with Mr. Cooper the science teacher.

Sibling Rivalry

"I'm looking forward to this Bernard," Mr. Cooper said, "I'm sure it will be excellent."

They entered the classroom and stopped suddenly. It took a while for Bernard to realise what he was looking at. The room was filled with an acrid, foul smelling cloud, there were bits of burnt paper floating in the air, and Bernard's models lay on the floor, each one broken into pieces.

"I......" Bernard couldn't speak.

"Do you know who did this?" Mr. Cooper asked, a hint of rage in his voice.

"No," Bernard answered quietly, secretly beginning to wonder whether his brother could be so wicked.

Several of Bernard's classmates pushed through the door.

"I'm afraid the presentations cancelled," Mr. Cooper herded them out of the classroom.

Bernard could hear them outside as Mr. Cooper explained what had happened. He sat down and held his head in his hands, he felt embarrassed by what had happened, everyone had seen his models strewn across the floor lying in pieces, they had all realised that Bernard wasn't as good as he, or his teacher, had thought. They now knew him as a failure and he didn't think he would ever be able to face them again. Mr. Cooper re-entered the classroom.

"Why don't you go home," he said softly, "I'll clean this up."

"That's all right, I'll help you." and together they picked up the bits of the models they could find and placed them in the bin as Bernard remembered how long he had spent making them and how carefully he had carried them to school. They washed out the sink and opened the windows to allow the smoke to clear. Finally it was all done and they left the school, Bernard said goodbye and slowly walked home thinking of how he would explain what had happened.

At home Samuel was waiting and he started to laugh at Bernard as soon as he walked into the house. This made Bernard realise he was the culprit and they had a terrible fight, it took all of their parents strength to separate the two boys and keep them apart.

Amy Alice and the Alchemists

They were sent to bed and in the morning Bernard explained what had happened. Samuel didn't try to deny it and was grounded for a month without any pocket money, this didn't bother him as he thought that it had been worth it to prevent his brother from getting even more praise.

The atmosphere in the Alice household went from bad to worse, especially when both twins were at home. They didn't speak, they didn't like to be in the same room together, they didn't even look at each other. They would still have their arguments and fights if one thought the other was being treated more favourably, especially Samuel who still felt very jealous of Bernard.

When they left school they both attended college and then went on to university to study science. They deliberately enrolled at different universities and avoided each other as much as they could. They were both top of their classes and gained the best grades in their exams but again Samuels jealousy was fuelled when he found out Bernard's marks were better than his and he wondered if he would ever better his brother at anything.

From university they went on to gain jobs, Bernard with a leading chemical company and Samuel worked for a laboratory specializing in the development of medicines used by vets on animals.

They went their separate ways and moved away from home. Bernard had opened his own chemists shop and been promoted to Master Alchemist within the guild, this had left Samuel furious as he had not been promoted so quickly. Samuel convinced Bernard's promising young apprentice Harris to leave Bernard's shop and work for him instead. The combination of Samuel's charm and the promise of great wealth had been too much for the young apprentice to ignore, however the future did not work out for Harris as he had expected. Samuel was a greedy man and worked his apprentice hard taking the credit for all of his new discoveries. Harris had become totally disillusioned with his new mentor and the life of an alchemist and disappeared from the guild never to be seen again. This infuriated Bernard, the young man had been very talented and his disappearance was a great loss to the guild, he swore he would never speak to his brother again.

Eavesdroppers and Vandals

It was about two days since Samuel had paid his visit and granddad was starting to relax a little as he had been quite quiet and thoughtful since he had seen his brother, as if something about the visit was bothering him. Amy didn't like to ask what was wrong, her granddad had been a little upset when he told her about Samuel and what he had gotten up to when they were growing up. But now granddad was almost back to his normal cheerful self.

Today granddad took Amy into the laboratory to find out what she was capable of doing since she had taken the magical potion.

"Ok Amy, do you think that you could change for me?"

"Of course, what would you like me to change into."

"Whatever you want." Granddad stood back and watched carefully as Amy started to shrink and turn from a little blond haired girl into a small woolly black sheep. Granddad was amazed, he still couldn't believe that this could happen. How was it possible? It wasn't scientifically possible, was it? Had he stumbled upon the greatest invention ever? Granddad was more and more excited the more he thought about it. He could be famous, he could be rich, but what about Amy?

Amy Alice and the Alchemists

Would the potion have some form of terrible side effects? Would she change into something and find she couldn't change back again? How would people treat her, and what would her parents say when they found out? All these questions raced around inside granddad's head as he took a tape measure and started to record Amy's height and length, he weighed her, looked deep into her eyes and ears and listened to her chest with a long stethoscope.

"Amy, can you hear me," he asked

"Yes," came the reply in a quiet voice.

"How do you feel?"

"It feels kind of straange at first, but you soon get uused to it," the Amy-sheep started to trot around the laboratory.

"Does it hurt when you change or while you are something different?"

"Not really, buuut I do feeel a liittle soorre the next day." granddad scribbled something down on his notepad.

"Can you change into something else now?"

"I'll try," the sheep started to change, it stood up on two legs and its curly black wool shrank except for the wool on its chin which grew longer and longer and changed from black wool to long white whiskers. Granddad couldn't believe it, in front of him now stood a stocky, rosy cheeked dwarf with a long white beard.

"How's that?" asked the dwarf.

"Amazing," gasped granddad, and again he went to work examining and recording everything about the dwarf, "I can't believe this, this is going to amaze the world. This could be my most brilliant potion ever, even better than the storm in a teacup potion."

He stood back, "I think that's enough, can you return to normal?"

Amy the dwarf became Amy the little girl again and granddad gave her a hug, "Are you sure you feel alright?" he asked as he looked at her eyes.

"Yes I feel fine, in fact it's quite exciting isn't it?"

Eavesdroppers and Vandals

"Oh it's exciting alright." a serious look came over his face before he continued. "But I still think we should keep it a secret for now, we don't want the wrong sort of people finding out about this, and we need to try to find some sort of antidote. I mean, we can't leave you like this for ever can we?" Granddad stood back and thought for a while, "What I need to know is why you change into these particular creatures. What do you think about to make you change?"

"I just think about something from a story and concentrate and it just happens."

"That will explain it!" granddads eyes shined brightly, "You keep changing into these creatures because it's your imagination which gives the potion its magical power. You can change into any fantastic creature you have ever read about in fairy tales or heard about in nursery rhymes because they are locked inside your imagination."

Amy thought about it and realised he was right, she had become the giant from Jack and the beanstalk, the bear was from Goldilocks and whilst she had been swimming in custard she must have been the frog prince.

"That's amazing granddad isn't it!"

"It certainly is amazing Amy but I'm afraid we can't leave you like this for ever. What is it doing to your body and what happens if you change into something and can't change back. I need to start working on an antidote." stooping over a dusty chest he began rummaging through a pile of papers. "I'm sure I left the recipe for the Doppelgangers Delight in here somewhere."

"What was that?" granddad asked suddenly. He listened carefully and thought he could hear footsteps outside.

Granddad raced out of the shed and stood looking around the garden. He caught a glimpse of a shadowy figure disappearing around the back of the shed and chased after it. As he turned around the corner of the shed he saw the figure on top of the garden wall for a split second before it dropped out of sight and could be heard running quickly away along the street.

Amy Alice and the Alchemists

"Who was it granddad?" Amy asked as she joined her granddad.

"I don't know," he answered as he surveyed the garden, "It doesn't look like they took anything."

"What do you think they were up to then?"

"I'm not sure," he looked up at the wall where he had last seen the figure and then looked along the side of the shed. A flower bed ran the length of the shed wall and he could see that several flowers had been flattened and trampled. He looked closer and found a small gap between the boards that made up the shed wall, when he looked through the hole he could see into the laboratory. His view was partially blocked by the leg of his workbench but he could see some of the interior of his lab.

He stood up and quietly walked back towards the shop locking the shed door on his way. Amy followed, she knew he was thinking carefully about the intruder and she wondered who it could have been. Why had they been there? What had they seen, what had they heard, and would they come back? Amy shivered as she entered the flat even though it was a warm afternoon. They sat in silence for a while before granddad turned to her.

"We'll have to work quickly Amy, we don't know what the intruder learned or if they might try to steal our secret and that worries me. It worries me most because you may be in danger! We need to be careful and if you see anyone acting strangely keep away and tell me as soon as you can, Ok?"

"Ok granddad, I promise," she was scared now and she wondered whether she would be in danger or if they were just over reacting and it had been a boy trying to pinch some of granddad's pears.

The next day Amy and her granddad went to the cinema, granddad thought that it would take her mind off what had happened the previous day. They had a great time, Amy loved the movie and granddad bought her popcorn and ice-cream, but it was soon time to leave and go home. When they arrived home granddad parked the car and they entered the shop.

Eavesdroppers and Vandals

"Would you like anything for tea?"

"No thank you," Amy replied. She was still full from the popcorn and ice-cream.

"I think I'll have a sandwich," granddad declared.

In the kitchen he started to make himself a sandwich but then suddenly stopped. Had he heard a noise from the garden? He wasn't sure, maybe it was just nerves because of what had happened the day before and he had just imagined it. No, there was definitely someone out there. Another loud crash could be heard coming from the bottom of the garden.

"Amy," he called "I want you to stay inside, don't come into the garden!" and he went out to see who was making the noise.

Amy was frightened, would granddad be ok, she hoped so. She didn't want him to get hurt, what should she do? She ran to the back door and turned the key, she felt a bit safer but the butterflies in her stomach were tumbling and churning around. She watched from the kitchen window as granddad tip-toed down the garden path.

As he crept along the path granddad felt the same as Amy, his stomach felt like it was full of butterfly's too. A loud crash came from the shed and he started to feel angry when he thought of all his work being destroyed. Leaning against the garden wall was a spade, granddad picked it up and held it out over his shoulder ready to protect himself from whoever was in the shed. He reached the shed door and waited, listening carefully he could hear someone inside rummaging around as if they were looking for something. Another loud crash echoed around the garden as the mystery vandal threw something to the floor. Granddad grew furious, he couldn't let them get away with it, that was his life's work they were ruining.

He kicked open the shed door and charged inside. Inside was a complete mess, there was broken glass every where, his books had been thrown around, the workbench had been toppled over, his boxes of tools had been emptied out on the floor in fact everything had been thrown around or broken, or both.

Amy Alice and the Alchemists

In the middle of all this mess stood a large figure with a box of nettle leaves in his hands. Granddad didn't know who he was, he had a black balaclava on his head which hid his face from sight. He was bigger than granddad and the black jumper he was wearing was tight around his broad shoulders and big stomach.

The vandal threw the box at granddad who just managed to avoid it, he then lunged at granddad who drew back the spade ready to strike the intruder.

Someone who had been hiding behind the shed door grabbed the spade and granddad was over powered by the first man before he had a chance to protect himself. Granddad was thrown to the floor and the mystery intruder landed heavily on top of him.

Thrashing around on the floor granddad surprised his attacker with his strength, they must have thought they were dealing with a weak old man but he had become enraged at the scene of devastation. He managed to turn himself around, grabbing at the figure and pulled the balaclava from his head.

The intruder was a stranger to granddad, he had never seen him before. He had a small thin moustache, his face was scarred and pitted, and his greasy black hair was pulled back into a tight pony tail. Granddad tired quickly as he struggled under the weight of his attacker and the intruder used this to his advantage forcing granddad over onto his front and pressing his face hard into the ground He was held in this position as the second intruder started to search the shed, all granddad could see from his place on the floor was their shiny black boots and dark black trousers.

"Where are the plans," whispered the one with the moustache as he pressed granddad further into the floor.

"What plans," grimaced granddad as he struggled to breath.

"You know, the formula that makes you change,"

"There is no formula. I don't know what you're talking about"

Eavesdroppers and Vandals

Granddad was trying hard to catch his breath, the weight of the man lying on him was making it harder and harder to breath and he was frightened he would soon pass out.

But who were these people, they weren't the one he had seen yesterday, that figure had been a lot smaller. Whoever had been eavesdropping had obviously told these two what he had heard and they thought they could become rich if they could steal the formula and find out how it worked. Suddenly the shed door burst open and the second intruder screamed.

Standing in the doorway was a short squat creature, it had green skin and long muscular arms that almost touched the ground. Its nose was long and fat and two of its teeth curled up and over its top lip.

"Oo's bin trip trappin on me granddad" it snarled huskily.

The second figure charged at the troll and caught it off guard, it barged past knocking the creature to the side and disappeared out of the shed. The Amy-troll looked at the disappearing figure and then back at the two men on the floor. Granddad had the feeling that it was taking the troll a long time to think about what it should do next and he could feel himself becoming feint from the weight pressing down on him.

Eventually the troll seemed to have an idea and strode over to them, it grabbed the intruder by the scruff of his jumper and dragged him away.

"Gerrof!" shouted the man as he struck out at the troll.

His blows bounced off the thick green hide and the troll kept on dragging him across the floor and out of the shed.

"If you fink you can trip trap on me granddad you need to be shown ow naughty you've bin"

The creature's short stumpy legs strode across the garden path, its big gnarled, hairy hand holding firmly onto the helpless vandal. When it had crossed the lawn and reached the garden pond it pushed the head of the helpless victim under the water and then lifted him out. The intruder gasped for breath.

Amy Alice and the Alchemists

"Don't ever come ere again" the troll spoke in a slow, dull drawl before pushing him under the water again.

The man found himself being pushed and pulled in and out of the water, he fought for breath and couldn't think of a way of escaping from this strong angry creature.

"I ope ive made meself clear," it snarled before plunging him once more into the small pond.

The gnarly creature dragged the gasping water logged figure over to the swing in the centre of the lawn. The man was dumped onto the grass as the troll uprooted the large double swing and started to snap off the legs as if they were tiny twigs. The bedraggled, bruised intruder tried to crawl away but was too exhausted and slumped to the floor. The troll picked him up and shoved one of the metal legs from the swing up the back of the mans jumper, it then grabbed one of the swings and wrapped it round and round the screaming figure, it did the same with the other swing and once finished the man was tied fast to the metal bar like a piece of meat on a skewer.

The troll carried the trussed up figure to the bottom of the garden, it lifted the man high above its head and then drove the stick into the ground. The man screamed and struggled but the bar held fast, the troll disappeared into the shed and came out with a piece of cloth which it shoved roughly into his mouth to stifle his screams.

Pressing its wart covered face close to its captives, its large bloodshot eyes glared at the terrified intruder. The overpowering smell of rotten fish seemed to fill the air.

"Roit, I wan you to tell me oo you are, an I dont wan you to start screaming again Ok, you soun just like a scardy-cat," the troll pulled the piece of cloth from the mouth of the wide eyed man.

The man screamed louder than ever.

The Amy-troll shoved the cloth back into his mouth.

"I'm gonna give you one more chance, I wanna know oo you are an why you're ear, an don't scream again or you'll be sorry." and again the troll removed the gag.

Eavesdroppers and Vandals

The man screamed again, "Help. Help!" he shouted at the top of his voice.

"Roit, I warned you," growled the troll, shoving the cloth back into his mouth.

The troll picked him up and strode back towards the pond with the man over one shoulder. At the top of the lawn it turned to face the wall at the bottom of the garden.

It lifted the struggling figure effortlessly above its head with one long hairy arm and started to run with short, heavy steps down the garden. Just before it reached the wall it launched the man into the air like a javelin with a great thrust of its powerful arm. The figure sailed over the garden wall and continued gaining height as it flew over the neighbouring gardens and disappeared out of sight.

The troll quickly changed back into Amy and she ran back to the shed to check on granddad. Granddad had climbed up off the floor and sat leaning against the wall his chest heaving in and out.

"Who were those people?" she asked as she crouched close to him. "He wouldn't tell me anything."

"I don't know," granddad gasped. "I've never seen him before, but at least they're gone now, thanks Amy you were brilliant."

Amy blushed, her cheeks burning, "Well they're gone for now"

"They'll be back," slowly he stood up, Amy held out her hand to help him, "Tomorrow I think we'll have to tell someone about you Amy, before they get a chance to do any more damage, or worse!"

"Who are you going to tell?"

"I'll inform the guild of what's happened."

"What's the guild?"

"It's a secret society of Alchemists, they'll be able to help, but you mustn't tell anyone about it, for all our sakes!"

"I understand."

After one final look at the devastated laboratory they slowly made their way back into the shop.

Amy Alice and the Alchemists

Another Meeting

Amy and her granddad were sat in granddad's battered red car traveling slowly, granddad was a very careful driver, along a winding country road. The road twisted and turned, fields and hedgerows bordered the narrow lane. Every now and then they would slow down to a snails pace as a car travelling in the opposite direction squeezed past, their wing mirrors barely missing each other, the bushes at the side of the road scraping noisily along Amy's door. They were far out into the countryside, there hadn't been sight of a house or a farm, or any type of building, for ages.

Amy was quite excited, this would be her first time at an Alchemists Guild meeting. That morning granddad had been on the telephone for hours, he called as many alchemists as he could get in touch with, an emergency meeting was hastily arranged to discuss the incident from the day before.

Granddads robes hung on a small hook in the back of the car. Amy had marveled at the intricate embroidery which depicted signs and symbols from the world of alchemy. She had caressed the soft fabric dreaming of the day when she would have a robe of her own.

Amy Alice and the Alchemists

I wonder if I'll ever get to wear the golden trim, she thought as she stroked the shiny silken under robe. As an apprentice she would have to wear grey trim but everyone has to start somewhere, even granddad had once worn the grey trimmed robes many years before.

"We will be arriving at DrakeDale very soon Amy." granddad spoke without taking his eyes from the road. "During the meeting I think it will be best if you wait in the car. There may be some negative things said and I don't want you to become alarmed. There are some stubborn, old fashioned alchemists in the guild and they can be quite rude."

Amy was disappointed now. She had been looking forward to discovering what went on in the meeting, watching the opening ceremony granddad had described to her in great detail, and seeing all the alchemists in their ceremonial robes.

Granddad hadn't wanted Amy to come, he had been worried at the thought of the reception she would receive and had asked her if she would stay with great uncle Percy, just for the day. Amy had become distraught at the thought of spending time with her disgusting relative and his grumpy dog. The thought of being given horrible jobs to do and having pet food for lunch made her feel quite sick. She had begged granddad to allow her to accompany him, eventually convincing him with a lot of tears that it would be better than leaving her with Percy. Granddad had given in at the sight of her becoming so upset, he reluctantly agreed to let her go with him.

After he had finished his telephone calls they had climbed into the car, a few false starts as granddad had to go back into the shop because he had forgotten his spectacles or he thought he had forgotten to lock the door, and they had begun their journey.

It was a long way to DrakeDale, granddad drove in silence all the way, tense and thoughtful, obviously rehearsing in his mind what he was going to say. Amy sat daydreaming through the window when she caught sight of a large house in the distance.

The DrakeDale Manor loomed larger and larger as they approached, a great imposing building situated at the bottom of a small hill.

Another Meeting

The car swung sharply to the right before stopping in front of a pair of huge decorative wrought iron gates depicting a flock of ducks flying up into the sky. The gates were attached to a high stone wall that disappeared along the road in both directions.

Granddad tapped some numbers on a small metal keypad fixed to the wall by the gate. Slowly the gates swung open allowing the car to drive through. Amy watched as they gently closed behind them, as they met she heard a small click and realised that she was now locked in. The car carefully followed a long driveway, the gravel crunching under the tyres. Tall trees bordered the drive on both sides, Amy could see great expanses of lawns with bushes cut into intricate shapes dotted everywhere. The drive opened out, the trees disappeared, in front of them was the largest house Amy had ever seen. It was three stories high and very, very long, Amy had never seen so many windows, there must have been hundreds of them. The front door was high and wide, an ivy clad roof supported by two ornate pillars cast the door in shadow.

Whoever lives here must be very rich, thought Amy as they passed a large pond with a fountain shooting water into the air. The pond was the home to a small group of brightly coloured ducks.

Granddad brought the car to a stop by the pond, climbing from the car he slipped his robes over his clothes before leaning in the open window.

"Don't worry, I won't be long. There are some sweets in the glove compartment, help yourself." He smiled sweetly, but Amy could tell that he was worried. He crossed the gravel drive before entering through the wide blue door.

Only three cars were parked on the gravel drive as granddad entered the manor house. Amy sat chewing on a toffee-fudge, watching as more cars arrived. The ducks had paddled across the pond, they were now waddling in and out of the cars quacking noisily, begging for food.

The occupants of the cars, who were all men, wore robes similar to granddads, Amy noticed that their robes were trimmed with either red or purple, not one of them wore the same golden trim as her granddad. One or two of the arrivals entered the building closely followed by younger men dressed in grey trimmed robes whom Amy guessed were apprentices.

Amy Alice and the Alchemists

As they passed the car the curious alchemists stared at Amy, frowning, wondering what a young girl was doing sat outside their rendezvous. She slumped down in her seat trying to hide from the gawping visitors, conscious of the fact that she was the only girl there.

Inside the hall Bernard stood at the head of the room in front of his high backed intricately carved chair. Samuel entered the room, without glancing at Bernard he took his seat beside another alchemist wearing the same purple trimmed robes as himself, immediately they fell into a hushed conversation. Bernard waited for the visitors to drift in, not as many people as he had hoped for took their seats. One of the last to enter was senior alchemist Unwin, he strode into the room with his nose in the air. Making his way to an unoccupied table at the front of the room he paused, surveying the other tables, checking on who had arrived, making sure everyone could see him. He nodded briefly to several people before settling into his seat to peer over his half moon spectacles at Bernard. Bernard acknowledged him with a quick nod before starting to speak, the room was barely half full.

"Gentlemen, thank you for attending at such short notice." his voice carried clearly across the room. "I have called you here to pass on some worrying news. Yesterday my laboratory was ransacked, two mysterious intruders broke in apparently searching for one of my new potions." he paused as questions were fired at him, motioning for calm before he continued. "I do not know who the intruders were, they were disturbed before they had found what they wanted and escaped." He would tell them about the Doppelgangers Delight and Amy's shape changing abilities, a little later.

"It is imperative that we all remain vigilant, these people could be involved with the disappearances of our colleagues and must not be underestimated."

"What makes you think they are involved?" a voice called from the back of the room. "If they had been, wouldn't they have kidnapped you as well?"

Another Meeting

"A fair assumption my friend, however as I have already mentioned the intruders were disturbed and fled from the scene empty handed. I am quite lucky to be stood here before you."

"Do you think you should have some form of guards at your shop just to be safe?" a short, fat, red robed alchemist asked.

"I do not think that will be practical, after all I may not be the only one in danger, we are all at risk and must remain alert to possible threats."

"If I may speak?" Senior Alchemist Unwin stood up as he spoke.

Bernard nodded, he sat back in his chair allowing Unwin to address everyone.

Unwin removed his half moon spectacles from his face before speaking, twiddling them between his fingers as he always did.

"If we had informed the police of the disappearances as I had requested then this mystery may have been resolved by now and we wouldn't be faced with worrying incidents such as this." he placed the end of the spectacles in his mouth contemplating on his next words.

"I was against the decision of giving the task to a mere boy. It is quite beyond his capabilities, I mean, where is he now? No one has heard from him since."

It was true, JP had disappeared. Maybe he had had second thoughts and decided not to search for the missing alchemists but was too ashamed to confess for fear of being branded a coward.

"However, now is the wrong time to take this further. Any interference from the police or ourselves could jeopardise the boy's safety. It will be better for all concerned to give him the benefit of the doubt and allow him the time to carry out his mission."

Unwin sat down, his head held high, an arrogant, smug look on his face.

"I agree." Bernard said, "These are wise words from our friend. I propose that we vote on the matter, green to allow the boy time, red to inform the police."

Amy Alice and the Alchemists

Whispered conversations could be heard around the room. Potions were mixed in the little silver cauldrons sat at the centre of each round table.

It wasn't long before several small green clouds floated above the heads of the alchemists.

"Very well, it is decided that the boy will be given time. I remind you that......"

"May I be so bold as to request further audience?" Unwin interrupted.

"Yes, certainly." Bernard reluctantly sat in his chair.

"We have lost three of our most cherished comrades," he faced the others in the room, his back to Bernard. "Their disappearance is a great burden for us all." his voice tinged with sadness. "I, more than anyone, would dearly love to see them back in their rightful place, but to be blunt, I do not think that we will see them for a long, long time. In fact we may never see them again. I would like to propose that we elect new committee members to take their seats." at this the room burst into life.

Shouts and catcalls mixed with calls of support were rained down upon Unwin who simply stood smiling, his glasses twisting and turning between his fingers.

"This is outrageous!" cried Bernard, "we cannot abandon our friends like this and elect others to take their place. I have every confidence that they will return to us unharmed and very soon. I will not contemplate the idea of electing a new council."

The majority of the alchemists in the room applauded this statement, calling "here, here" and "well said", as Bernard stood glowering at Unwin.

Unwin didn't seemed fazed by the reaction to his statement. He took his seat calmly, replacing his spectacles he peered over them at Bernard.

This is certainly the wrong time to tell them about Amy, he thought, he never dreamed he would ever think it but maybe some of his colleagues weren't to be trusted. Unwins' statement had him deeply worried.

Another Meeting

"If there is no one else who would like to speak then I would like to close this meeting." the anger and resentment in his voice could clearly be heard. "I thank you all for attending at such short notice, remember we must all remain vigilant and we must all stick together." he stared at Unwin as he spoke these last words.

Everyone filed from the room discussing what had been said. Unwin was the first to leave, he strode out of the hall his robes billowing out behind him. He avoided speaking to anyone, looking at the floor as he left the room, trying to hide the wicked almost contented smile that had formed at the corners of his mouth.

Bernard slumped in his chair as he watched his colleagues leave silently, he couldn't believe the audacity of Unwin, how could he be so heartless as to abandon his friends at a time like this?

Samuel was one of the last to leave, as he stood up he looked directly at Bernard, without smiling he nodded at his twin, made a motion which Bernard translated as an invitation to give him a call and then disappeared into the crowd.

Amy Alice and the Alchemists

Shadows Return

During the journey home granddad was just as quiet as he had been earlier. He sat brooding about something and Amy didn't know whether she should ask him or not. She decided it would be best to leave him with his thoughts, so she sat gazing out of the window watching the fields and hills flashing by, lost in her own thoughts about how she would become normal again (or if she really wanted to become normal). She had enjoyed having these special powers, it had filled her with a confidence she had never felt before. She had the ability to overcome any obstacle put before her, her whole outlook had changed. Where before she had been the victim of a callous bully, a timid, quiet girl, now she was a strong, brave girl. She had stood up to her tormentor and she had defeated the intruders that had destroyed granddad's laboratory.

Back home they busied themselves cleaning the damaged laboratory. Most of the equipment was beyond repair and had to be discarded.

Amy Alice and the Alchemists

The doppelganger plant, which at the moment was a pink rose, lay on the floor, Amy placed it on one of the few remaining shelves. She was pleased to see that the jar of leeches remained intact, the black ribbon-like worms swam lazily through the water patiently waiting for their next meal. They worked till late clearing up as much as they could before retiring to bed.

Amy lay restlessly in bed, she tossed and turned, finding it impossible to get to sleep. Pictures of black clad figures rushed through her head, their faces distorted, their identities unknown. Eventually she fell into a troubled sleep, dreaming vividly, muttering to herself about saving the animals.

She woke with a start, staring up at the ceiling she wondered what had woken her. She tried to recall her dream, had she woken because of a nightmare? It was possible. Then she heard it, a floorboard creaked outside her bedroom door.

A dark figure emerged from granddads bedroom followed by the zombie like shadow that was Bernard Alice. Bernard walked dreamily, his eyes fastened on the shiny blue crystal held out before his face. The dark stranger led him to the top of the stairs, a floorboard creaked, the noise amplified in the silent house. The figures head spun quickly to another shadow which had appeared from the bedroom. They stopped, staring at each other, their eyes wide through the slits of their dark balaclavas. The first kidnapper motioned with a nod of its covered head towards Amy's bedroom. The second, larger figure tiptoed towards the room where the little girl was sleeping.

The bedroom door slowly swung open, the mysterious, dark silhouette crept towards the sleeping figure in the bed. With a violent tug the bedclothes were whipped away to reveal pillows placed where the girl should have been. He threw the blankets to the floor, searching under the bed he became angry, frustrated at her disappearance. He stormed over to the open window, peering out carefully to ensure he wasn't spotted he searched for the girl but again there was no sign of her.

The girl had gone!

Shadows Return

He scratched his head, she couldn't just disappear, there was nowhere to go, she wasn't in the room that was for sure and the window was too high to jump from. Through the narrow slit of the balaclava the dark eyes narrowed as they searched the room looking for a likely hiding place. Tiptoeing over to the wardrobe he thrust the doors open but again there was no sign of her. He felt like screaming with anger but he knew he must remain silent, no one must know they were here.

Tiptoeing out of the room he shrugged his shoulders, palms out to inform his partner that she had gone. Again, without saying a word they led Bernard down the stairs. A coat and hat were given to the chemist and he dutifully put them on, any thoughts of resistance far away in the deep recesses of his mind, his concentration solely on the crystal.

They crossed the shop floor. Opening the door they checked the dark street, all was quiet as they stepped out closing the door gently behind them. Moving down the street they crept from one shadow to the next, leaving the safety of the shop behind them, heading off into the dark unknown.

Amy watched them from the rooftop of the shop. When she had heard the floorboard creak she had climbed out of bed, after rearranging her pillows she opened the window and sat on the windowsill looking out at the high street. Amy quickly changed herself into a large black spider and scuttled effortlessly up the drainpipe onto the roof. Half hidden in the gutter she listened for any sounds coming from her bedroom. Shortly after she had escaped she heard someone rummaging around inside obviously looking for her. The sounds of searching stopped, seconds later footsteps could be heard on the pavement below. Amy stretched her long hairy legs to peer over the edge of the gutter. She watched as the three figures disappeared into the night.

The spider grew larger, its eyes became large round saucers, little feathery tufts which looked like ears sprouted from its head. Six of its eight legs moulded together to form wings, while its remaining legs developed scales and sharp talons on its feet.

Amy Alice and the Alchemists

The owl spread its wings, it rose up into the dark night sky. Unused to flying Amy wobbled unsteadily from side to side, her wings moving in an uncoordinated, haphazard fashion. Flapping her wings in a panic she tried to prevent herself from falling to the ground but she was losing height rapidly. The ground was hurtling towards her. She flapped her great wings harder trying to slow her descent but the floor was approaching at an alarming rate. Just as she thought she was going to hit the pavement she gained control and hovered close to the ground a short way behind granddad and his abductors. Her soft wings flapped silently in the air making sure she wasn't heard, she watched as they continued walking away from her, unaware of her presence.

With a huge beating of her wings she rose up into the air the wind ruffling her feathers. Amy had never felt as free as she flew silently over the heads of the strangers leading her granddad away. The exhilarating feeling of soaring so high gave Amy the greatest, most memorable experience she had ever had. She didn't want to come down, she wanted to fly for ever. She circled over the heads of the people far below, rising up higher and higher before swooping down. Amy was really enjoying herself but then reality surged back to take control forcing her to concentrate on what was happening. She flew over to a large tree finding a perch on a thick gnarled branch.

The large round eyes of the owl could see the figures clearly in the dark, she watched as they bundled granddad into a funny orange van. The van resembled a small caravan, windows ran along its sides each one dressed with a short tatty curtain which was drawn preventing anyone from discovering its contents. A large spare tyre was fastened to the front of the van, like a big black nose, giving it a quaint old fashioned look.

The van started to roll quietly down the bank, its engine silent. It moved away slowly gradually building up speed as it made its way down the steep hill. At the bottom of the slope the engine kicked into life. The van, with granddad inside, headed out of the village. The ghostly grey owl floated high above it, its soft grey feathers totally silent as it soared effortlessly through the night sky. The owl followed the van out onto a lonely country lane.

Shadows Return

The road twisted and turned, snaking through fields and meadows. It crossed a small hump backed bridge spanning a lazy stream. At one point it disappeared into a tunnel, the owl hovered overhead patiently waiting for it to emerge from beneath the rail track. The van continued its journey, the road curved round the base of a large hill before passing through a small village. Driving quickly past a row of small thatched cottages the van left the village, a short time later the owl watched as the van entered a small farm yard. It drove slowly along the dirt track before disappearing into a decrepit old barn.

The Amy-owl found a vantage point in a tree growing in the field opposite the creepy looking farm. The buildings were derelict, some of the windows were broken, tiles were missing from the roof and a tangled mass of ivy had been allowed to roam wildly over the front of the building.

The Amy-owl didn't dare enter the dark barn, she would wait to see what would happen next.

Amy Alice and the Alchemists

The Owl and the Pussycat

Renshaw was a tiny village situated at the bottom of a large hill. The village itself consisted of a single row of cottages, all thatched with straw and each one immaculately presented with lovely floral displays and neat green lawns. At one end of the road stood the village church, a small ancient chapel with a bell that kept time every quarter of an hour and the odd gravestone dotted here and there within the grounds. At the opposite end of the village was the local post office, a tiny little place which was used by the locals for mail, as a shop and as a meeting place to share gossip.

The people who lived in Renshaw had all lived there for many years and everyone knew everyone else. They all attended church every Sunday and would meet once a month in the church hall for the village meeting. The village meetings always consisted of the same topic, keep strangers out of Renshaw. They had managed to do this by putting off anyone who showed an interest in moving there and encouraging relatives of locals to join them. The village had, therefore, become a very close knit and secretive place where strangers were very rarely seen.

Amy Alice and the Alchemists

For the last six months the village had been buzzing with new gossip about the farm. The farm had been empty for years since old man Johnson had died and was now virtually derelict, but lately a van had been seen coming and going every couple of weeks and a new sign had been put up telling people to keep away. The villagers weren't happy about this as they hadn't been aware that someone had bought it and whoever it was hadn't shown their faces. The village meetings now consisted of rumours about who the mystery new resident could be.

Renshaw farm was an old unused farmhouse on the outskirts of the village, the farm buildings had been allowed to fall to bits, ravaged by year after year of neglect. The gate which opened onto the farmyard was hanging forlornly from the stump of a gate post, the fence which had once been attached had disappeared long ago. What looked like a new sign had been stuck into the ground by the side of the gate, "Private Property. Keep Out" it read in large red letters. From the gate the muddy track wound between two creepy looking barns, cobwebs hung from the corners of the doorways and the deep shadows inside were only investigated by the bravest of the villagers. Once past the barns the track crossed a weed infested farmyard to the door of the farmhouse. The house was a large stone building, the blue paint on the door was flaking and faded but the door itself still looked secure and forbidding. The four windows looking out over the farmyard were grimy and along with the grey tattered curtains prevented any unwanted prying.

The Amy-owl sat on the branch of a tree across the road from the farm and watched as the kidnappers led granddad from the barn and walked up the path to the farmhouse. Granddad stumbled across the farmyard his eyes still transfixed on the diamond which twisted and turned on its golden chain. Avoiding the potholes in the dirt track they made their way to the door of the farmhouse, the largest of the strangers took a key from his pocket and after unlocking the door they disappeared inside.

The Owl and the Pussycat

The owl flew the short distance across the road and landed on the dirt track between the two barns. The openings to the barns looked forbidding, cobwebs spanned the corners and the dark interior made the doorways look like huge black mouths waiting to swallow her up. She thought she heard something move deep inside the dark interior of the deserted barn, a shiver ran down her back and she quickly hopped along the track between the barns and was relieved when she had passed them and stood in the yard.

The yard was covered with weeds and had pot-holes dotted everywhere. To her left stood a tiny brick building, the door was missing and inside Amy could see a dirty old toilet, at the other end of the yard stood the house. Amy looked up at the house, she couldn't see inside as the windows were too dirty, she felt a little spooky as she looked up at it and she had an awful feeling that someone was stood behind the dirty grey curtains watching her every move.

She new granddad was inside but she had to find a way of getting in without being found out. Trying the door wasn't an option in case the kidnappers heard her, she would have to find another way to get inside and discover what was happening. Looking up at the house she realised that the roof was quite badly damaged with slates missing everywhere. The Amy-owl spread her wings and flew up quickly to find a precarious perch on a piece of loose gutter. Amy sat opposite a large hole where a slate had once been, she took a deep breath and pushed her way through.

She found herself in a large attic room, the room was dark but it didn't take long for the Amy-owl's eyes to become accustomed to the murky interior. The gaps in the roof which had been created by the missing slates allowed beams of early morning light to filter through. They had obviously allowed the rain to invade the space too as large damp patches could be seen all over the floor.

As she looked around Amy could smell the damp and she could see everything was covered in a thick layer of dust. Everywhere she looked there were cobwebs, they hung from the rafters, they spanned the corners and they covered the bare light bulb hanging in the centre of the room.

Amy Alice and the Alchemists

It was obvious that this room hadn't been used for a long time. The attic was empty apart from a cracked mirror leaning against the wall, and three large rusty cages that looked like they had once been the home for pet mice or guinea pigs.

At the end of the room stood a door, Amy changed back into herself and tiptoed over, taking hold of the handle she slowly turned it. The door opened reluctantly and Amy peeked through the gap she had created. Stairs ran down away from the attic to the floor below.

I'll need to be able to see clearly, thought Amy, and also move around silently so as not to be discovered. Amy changed herself into a cat, the cat was completely black except for a white patch over its left eye, she could see to the bottom of the stairs and when she started her descent her soft paws were silent on the old wooden boards. At the bottom of the stairs she found herself on a large landing.

The landing ran the length of the house, a spindled banister opened onto the top of the staircase which ran down to the hallway below. Amy guessed that the doors on either side lead into bedrooms but because of the spooky feel of the house she was reluctant to look inside. The smell of mould and dampness was strong here too, the walls were streaked with water from the attic above and the wallpaper was hanging limply. Amy listened carefully, hearing nothing but her own heartbeat in her ears she made her way along the landing to peer down to the ground floor. Again Amy waited, listening for any signs of life below.

If Amy hadn't seen the kidnappers enter the house herself she would have thought that the place was empty. There wasn't a sound, it was totally silent and Amy feared that at any moment a dark figure would charge from his hiding place and pounce on her. She took a deep breath and, her heart pounding, she started down the stairs step by step. Each time she tenderly placed her foot on a stair she cringed expecting the old timber steps to creak and groan under her weight, but thankfully she reached the floor without a sound.

The Owl and the Pussycat

The passageway she now stood in ran from the staircase to the front door, halfway along the hall were doors one on either side. Immediately to her right was another door which was open and Amy could see led into a large kitchen, she peeked round the corner of the door frame and found the room empty. Inside, the kitchen was again in a state of disrepair, the cupboard doors hung from their hinges, if they weren't missing altogether, the stove looked dirty and unused and cobwebs covered the windows. On top of the stove Amy noticed a kettle which stood out from the rest of the house simply because it was clean, then she realised that the sink was clean too as if someone had recently scrubbed it. The table in the corner was also spotless and then Amy noticed a brand new refrigerator hidden behind one of the broken cupboard doors.

Amy tiptoed over to the fridge, quickly changing back into herself she opened the fridge and looked inside, it was crammed with food. There were pies, cheese, fruit and meat, all kinds of delicious looking things and Amy's tummy rumbled at the sight of them. The kidnappers must use this place quite often, and they had obviously stocked up with food when they had planned their abduction. Amy resisted the temptation to eat something and closed the door. She changed back into the cat before anyone caught her, it would be a lot safer she thought

There were three doors leading from the kitchen, the one Amy had entered through, a large heavy door that led out to the back of the house and another door that was split into two like those seen on a stable. The Amy-cat leapt up to balance on the stable door and peered over the closed lower half.

For an animal lover like Amy what she saw almost made her sick and she was pleased that she hadn't eaten anything from the fridge because she was sure it would have come straight back up again.

The room she was looking into was the old butcher's room where the farmer would slaughter the animals before he sold the meat at market. A huge sturdy looking bench filled the centre of the room, the heavy wood top stained dark from blood.

Amy Alice and the Alchemists

A row of vicious looking metal hooks hung from the ceiling, a dark stain on the floor below each one, and along the far wall a rack with two rusty knives and an old lethal looking cleaver still remained.

Amy could virtually smell the blood in the room and she imagined the fear that the poor animals must have felt before they were slaughtered, she quickly turned away and dropped back down onto the kitchen floor fighting back the tears of sorrow she now felt.

Suddenly she heard a loud bang from the butcher's room and she fled in terror back into the hall and up the stairs, trying her hardest to move quickly without making a noise. She hid around the corner of the landing making sure she had an escape route into the attic but with a clear view of the hall below. She could hear someone in the kitchen moving around, opening and closing cupboard doors. Then she heard another great thud and the house was silent again. Amy gave herself a little time to recover from her fright before she made her way back down the stairs and into the kitchen. She took a deep breath and steadied herself before she could manage to look back into that awful room and this time she saw something she had missed the first time.

Behind the table, set into the floor, was a trapdoor. This must have been where the noise came from that startled Amy, the kidnappers must be in the cellar and they must have granddad down there! Amy started to panic, she needed to get down there to save granddad and she needed to do it without getting caught herself, but how?

The little black cat sat on the cold kitchen floor contemplating her next move. Her ears pricked and she froze, what was that? She was sure she had heard something. There it was again, a dull, rasping, grinding sound, she listened hard, it was coming from the kitchen window. As she watched she saw the dirty, grimy window inch slowly upwards, bit by bit it rose squeaking and groaning as it went. Amy was confused, how was it opening? She couldn't see anyone but it still continued to slowly rise.

The Owl and the Pussycat

The window was now half open and had stopped moving when Amy thought she saw something move, she blinked her eyes, it couldn't be, but then it happened again. It appeared that a part of the wall outside had crept through the window, a part of the wall which looked leg shaped to be exact, but then it disappeared again and all Amy could see was the window and the rusty old sink. The Amy-cat thought she could sense someone in the room, her heightened senses could smell them, she could hear their breathing, but she couldn't see them. Something moved, a shimmering, translucent shadow, but when Amy looked closer the figure had disappeared again. Whoever it was they were moving towards Amy, she could feel them getting closer and closer but she couldn't move, she was frozen with fear. Unaware of who or what they were, unaware of what they would do, unaware of when they would strike, she waited.

She waited until she thought she was going to burst with fright aware that whatever it was, it was right beside her when it took her completely by surprise.

"Nice puss," it whispered, "No need to be afraid, I'm just looking for Master Alice. You run along now, go on, out you go, the windows open."

Amy couldn't believe it, "Master Alice!" it must have meant granddad, but who else would be here in a deserted farmhouse looking for her granddad?

She followed him back into the hall, the unseen person was moving very slowly, step by step he crept along the hall the faint sound of his breathing the only clue as to his whereabouts.

As she watched Amy thought she saw a faint outline appear, a misty silhouette. The figure became more defined, the wallpaper framed by the shimmering outline was being replaced by the features of a young boy. A blurred image of a heavy green coat became darker and darker, dirty blue jeans came into focus and then a mop of greasy brown hair appeared until finally a freckled, dirt smudged face completed the picture. The cat and the boy stood staring at each other along the length of the hallway.

Amy Alice and the Alchemists

JP

The Amy-cat cocked it's head to one side as it studied the boy. He appeared to be older than Amy, about 14 or 15 maybe, but not very tall, quite short in fact. He looked very dirty, as if he hadn't been washed for days, his face and hair were covered with dirt and dust and his clothes were stained and grubby. He watched the cat watching him.

"You can see me can't you?" he whispered, obviously not expecting an answer.

The cat nodded.

The boy shook his head, he must have imagined it.

He looked at his hands, "Yes, you can definitely see me now." he sounded a bit disappointed.

The boy took a small bottle from one of the many pockets on his coat and examined it, "I don't have much left, I'll have to use it carefully."

He replaced the bottle in his pocket, from a different pocket he pulled out a small yellow plastic gun. He held the gun out in front of him like someone in an American cop show and made his way quietly back to the foot of the stairs where the cat was sitting. He stroked the cat gently.

Amy Alice and the Alchemists

"I know master Alice is in here somewhere," he whispered, "and it's my job to find him." he looked up the stairs, "I think I'll start up there." and he slowly crept up the stairs, the plastic gun held out stiffly in front of him.

Amy was relieved that she now had an ally to help her find granddad but what he thought he could do with a water pistol was anybody's guess, mind you he had been invisible to start with and that little trick could turn out to be a big help.

The big question on Amy's mind was who was he and how had he known granddad was here. He must be an Alchemist because he had called granddad "Master Alice" and the little bottle must have contained a potion. But that didn't answer the question of how he new granddad was here. There was only one thing for it, Amy would have to ask him.

The Amy-cat watched the boy disappear up the stairs, once he was out of sight she quickly changed back into herself. She wanted to ask him who he was but she thought a talking cat would be too much for him to handle, even if he could make himself invisible.

She crept up the stairs after him, she had to be quiet as she didn't want to startle him, and there was always the kidnappers to worry about, she didn't want them finding out they were here.

Amy reached the landing but the boy was gone.

"Hello," she whispered, conscious of those not so nice people hiding down stairs, "it's me Amy Alice, I'm looking for my granddad too."

She crept along the landing to the first door. Taking hold of the handle she slowly turned it and pushed the door open a fraction. The door creaked and Amy glanced nervously towards the stairs, hearing nothing she peered through the gap. The room was dark and dingy, she scanned it quickly but there was no sign of the boy hiding in the shadows. Amy crept further along the landing and checked inside another empty damp room, she closed the door and turned to face the last remaining door at the end of the landing.

Taking hold of the handle she carefully opened the door and slowly pushed it open. Light filtered through the small dirty window, a stained grimy toilet stood next to a broken basin. Along the opposite wall stood an old rusty bathtub, inside the bathtub crouched the boy.

JP

"D,don't c,c,come any c,closer," he stuttered nervously as he pointed the water pistol at Amy, "or I'll, I'll...." his voice trailed off to silence.

Amy pushed the door open wider and stepped into the dark room.

"Hi, don't shoot I'm on your side," she held her hands out hoping to appear friendly, "I'm looking for Master Alice too, I'm his granddaughter."

The boy peered through the gloom at Amy, the water pistol still aimed at her.

"Amy?" he asked.

"Yes its me." she stepped forward.

He sat up in the bathtub, his eyes opened wide with recognition.

"What are you doing here? I didn't see you leave the shop."

After checking the landing to make sure they hadn't been heard Amy closed the bathroom door. She was puzzled now and asked, "What do you mean you didn't see me leave the shop. What shop?"

"Your granddads, I've been watching it every night for the past two weeks and I saw the kidnappers take Master Alice away but I didn't see you with them. How did you get here so fast?"

"Never mind that," she didn't want to tell a complete stranger about her special ability, not just yet. "Why were you watching the shop?" and as an afterthought, "And who are you anyway?"

The boy stood up, he stuck out his chest and tried to make himself appear confident and important.

"My name is Jonathan Polldown, although every one calls me JP. I am an apprentice of the grey order of the Secret Guild of Alchemists." he spoke in a very posh almost forced accent, "Your grandfather, Master Alchemist Alice of the gold order, gave me the honorable task of investigating the mysterious disappearances of the Master Alchemists." he stepped out of the bath and tried to look down his nose at Amy as he spoke. "Very brave, that's what your granddad said. The most competent and able person to take on such a dangerous task." he puffed out his chest, "But that didn't frighten me, I wasn't worried at all. I know I can find out who these kidnappers are and rescue them all."

Amy Alice and the Alchemists

Amy wasn't totally convinced, she thought his boasting was a little forced, false bravado hiding a nervous young boy. However she was pleased he was here all the same, any help would be better than none, and the two of them together would have a better chance of rescuing granddad, even if one of them was only armed with a water pistol!

"Did you just say that more Alchemists had disappeared?" Amy asked.

"Yes, your granddad is the fourth Master Alchemist in two years to disappear. Didn't you know?"

"No, granddad didn't tell me." probably to stop me from worrying she thought to herself.

"Like I say, I was given the dangerous, enviable task of discovering who was behind the disappearances and why our most senior colleagues seemed to just vanish into the night."

"Well do you think we should try and find my granddad?" she was becoming bored with his delusions of grandeur. "I've searched the house and there's no sign of them but I did hear someone going into the cellar so they must be down there. You could become invisible again and sneak down."

"Er.... I don't know..... You see......" he seemed a bit unsure of himself, his confident manner slightly ruffled. "I can't actually make myself invisible."

"But when I was hiding downstairs you just appeared from nowhere!"

"I wasn't invisible I was camouflaged." he held out the small bottle which was almost empty. "This is a potion created by the alchemist I am apprentice to, I sort of borrowed it." he said sheepishly, "It's called Calmer Chameleon, a few drops on your head and you blend in with your surroundings so you can't be seen."

"I see, well you might as well be invisible it's just as good."

JP

"There's just one drawback, to make sure you stay hidden when you move the potion only allows you to move very, very slowly. It sort of calms you down to a snails pace."

Amy now understood why she thought she had caught glimpses of him when he had climbed through the kitchen window, it must have taken the potion a few seconds to adjust to the interior of the house.

"I used it while I was watching your granddad's shop," JP continued, "and when the kidnappers went inside I hid in their van. But I couldn't save Master Alice then because the potion was making me move too slowly, I just had to sit there and wait. I couldn't even tell him I was there or I would have been heard."

Amy felt sorry for him, so close to saving granddad but powerless to do anything, it must have been very frustrating.

"I don't have much left." he was studying the bottle again, "I'm going to need to make some more, it could come in useful."

"Does that mean you need to find a laboratory?" Amy stated the obvious.

"Yes, but I'm sure we passed a small chemist shop in the village. There'll be a lab hidden in there and the owner will be a member of the guild, he'll be able to help us and call for help." his confident manner had returned. "I say we go there first and stock up on some potions to help us."

Amy wasn't sure, she wanted to go straight down stairs and confront the kidnappers, with her powers she would be able to save granddad alone. However, it would be safer with two of them, having some potions would help a lot, and what if there were more kidnappers waiting down there, she had seen two enter the house but that didn't mean there weren't more already in the cellar. She debated for a while on the best course of action and then decided it would be better to stick together although she would keep her magical doppelganger like powers to herself for a while, just until it was really necessary to tell him, just to make sure she could trust him fully.

"Ok, we'll go to the shop, but let's do it quickly so we can get back here before anything happens to granddad."

"Right follow me, and keep the noise down," Amy wasn't keen on his bossy manner.

They crept down the stairs, JP holding his water pistol out in front of him pointing it at every doorway and shadowy corner they passed.

Amy giggled to herself, he looked ridiculous holding the water pistol out like that, but if it made him feel braver then let him carry on.

They tiptoed down the stairs and quietly made their way into the kitchen. JP watched the doorway to the butcher's room as Amy climbed out of the window. Once she was safely outside JP followed her and carefully closed the window. They crouched down out of sight. The sun wasn't fully up yet and it was still quite dark.

"Why didn't you just use the door?" Amy asked suspiciously.

"I, err, I tried but it wouldn't work." He didn't sound too convincing.

Maybe he just likes pretending to be some sort of super-hero. Amy wondered what would happen when he really did have to be brave.

"We need to get to the main road without being seen but I don't have enough Calmer Chameleon for both of us." JP whispered, "Anyway it would slow us down too much. I'll go first and run to the back of the outhouse, when I give the signal you follow me."

Running as fast as they could they made their way one by one from the back of the farmhouse to the outhouse, then to the barn and finally to the gate at the bottom of the lane. Crossing the road they pushed their way through the small hedge and hid in the field opposite. They sat in the shadow of the old oak and waited for their chests to stop heaving in and out from their scrambled sprint. As soon as they had recovered they set of walking the short distance to the village. Trudging through the soft earth at the edge of the field they were shielded from the road by the hedgerow.

Hiding behind a bush JP pointed out the chemist shop. It was a door which appeared to be wedged between two cottages, there were no windows and as far as Amy could see no way of telling that this was a chemist shop, or any type of shop for that matter.

JP

"How do you know it's a chemist shop?" she asked.

"The sign above the door," he pointed it out.

Above the door was a small triangular sign. In each corner of the triangle was an Alchemical symbol which Amy recognized, it was exactly the same as the one which hung above granddads shop door.

"Come on," said Amy, she was eager to get back to the farm, "let's hurry up."

They crossed the road and made their way to the shop. The white door was locked solid and a small sign had been screwed to the wall.

Renshaw Village Chemist Shop
For all your medicinal needs
please visit our website at :
www.chemistdirect/mednet.com
24 hour delivery guaranteed

"Its shut," JP couldn't believe it, "I hope the labs still intact. Keep watch!"

Please would be nice thought Amy as she watched the deserted street. JP pulled a bottle from one of his pockets and poured a couple of drops onto the lock. The droplets moulded together and formed a small pool. As JP watched, the liquid sausage crept, caterpillar like, deep into the lock. They waited for what felt like hours, expecting a nosy neighbour to appear at any minute. After a short wait they heard the telltale click which told them the door was open, a quick glance up and down the street to make sure they weren't being watched and they stepped inside.

"Open sesame potion?" Amy asked.

"Yeah, another one I borrowed just in case."

As they looked into the deserted building they realised that they were now stood in what had to be the smallest chemist shop in the world!

103

Amy Alice and the Alchemists

The Old Shop

As they entered the front door of the tiny shop it only took two steps and they were stood at the counter. The shop was very narrow, there was just enough room for them to stand side by side. The interior was dark and dingy, a small skylight in the roof allowed some light into the room but it took a while for their eyes to become accustomed to the dimness.

It was obvious that the shop wasn't being used at present as the long row of shelves behind the counter were bare save for the odd bottle or jar which had been left to collect dust.

The shelves behind the counter lined one wall of a long narrow corridor like space which ended with a wooden door. Apart from the skylight there were no windows and no more doors. It was just a long thin room with one door in and one door out.

JP lifted a portion of the counter and stepped through followed by Amy.

"It's not what I was expecting." he said disappointedly. "I was hoping for a fully stocked shop so I could make some potions."

"The lab may have some things you could use." Amy said hopefully.

"If we can find it," he led the way towards the back of the shop. The narrow gangway ended in the door and JP opened it tentatively.

He was confronted by a cupboard, a row of shelves were fitted to the back wall but apart from that it was completely empty.

JP tapped on the walls, he pulled at the shelves, he opened and closed the door time after time but the cupboard remained unchanged.

"There must be another way out, a secret door to the lab. It's got to be here somewhere."

He couldn't understand it, there were no nooks or crannies in the shop to hide a secret door, it must be here in the cupboard.

"Try some open sesame potion." Amy suggested half heartedly.

"I suppose anything's worth trying," he replied.

JP took the small bottle from his pocket and poured a couple of drops onto one of the shelves. He waited patiently, Amy stood on her tiptoes and craned her neck to watch over his shoulder. It was obvious to them that nothing was going to happen, the drops of liquid sat unmoving on the dusty shelf.

They both sighed disappointedly, it was starting to appear that the lab was too well hidden.

"Maybe there isn't a lab here, I mean the shop is a bit small, and it isn't even used anymore."

"There must be one, you saw the sign outside. Every single chemist shop has a secret Alchemists laboratory hidden somewhere." he was beginning to become annoyed at not being able to find it, Amy would start having doubts about his ability as an Alchemist.

"Tell you what, you start at that end and I'll start here and we'll make sure we search every inch of this place. Look for a switch or a door or anything that looks unusual."

He started tapping on the wall as Amy walked back to the front of the shop. Just as she reached the counter someone hammered loudly on the front door. Amy ducked quickly behind the counter and turned to see JP dive into the cupboard and slam the door shut.

The Old Shop

"Are you sure you saw someone Mildred?" a voice called from outside, "The door hasn't been forced and it's still locked solid."

He knocked again even louder and Amy cringed as she cowered behind the counter.

"There's no answer Mildred and I can't hear anything." a pause, Amy thought she could hear someone else speaking but it was very faint as if they were far away.

"There's no point, the place is empty!" he sounded like he was losing his patience. It went quiet for a second and then she heard the sound of footsteps receding.

She stood up and tiptoed to the back of the shop.

"JP, they've gone you can come out now." She whispered towards the cupboard door.

No answer.

"JP, can you hear me?"

Again, no answer.

Amy slowly opened the cupboard door.

JP was gone!

He must have found the secret door she thought excitedly as she stepped into the cupboard. Amy closed the door behind her, it was tiny and she had to squeeze herself in to get the door closed. She felt quite claustrophobic, the dust tickled her nose and the smell of medicine was strong in the confined space.

As soon as the door closed the back wall of the cupboard swung open to reveal a dark narrow staircase. Intrigued, Amy tried opening the cupboard door, the secret door clicked tight shut. As she closed the cupboard door the secret door again swung open, whoever had designed this must have been really small she thought as she stood crammed into the space, if she had been any bigger she wouldn't have been able to get the door closed.

Amy Alice and the Alchemists

Amy made her way cautiously down the stairs, a soft flickering light illuminated the steps which were narrow and steep. She took her time in the gloomy space and safely reached the bottom where she stepped out into the light.

JP stood in the centre of the deserted laboratory. The flickering glow was cast by a single ever burning light which hung crookedly on one wall. The low ceiling and shadowy corners made the narrow room feel very small and creepy. Most of the equipment that JP needed had been removed. There were no bellows, no cauldron, no chemicals, no recipe book, nothing that a good Alchemist would normally have.

JP's heart sank, how would he be able to work with this, all that was left was a few rusty old tins, a handful of half empty bottles on one shelf, their labels faded and browned, and a box containing some withered plants. In the far corner stood a small fireplace, a few twigs lay scattered around, a small table lay on its side in the centre of the room.

JP's started to gather his senses.

"We'll need some water," he said, "take those tins to the pond we passed in the field and bring some back."

Bossy, bossy, bossy thought Amy.

"Collect some grass, some soil, a stone, and some leaves, and get back here as soon as you can."

"And what will you be doing?" came the frosty reply.

"I'll be making a fire and sorting out what's still useful out of this lot," he said glancing around the room.

JP handed her the open sesame potion as Amy picked up a couple of dented tins and climbed the stairs back up to the shop.

Waiting at the front door she listened for any signs of the neighbours but all was silent. Peeping out she saw that it was now deserted, and taking the opportunity of a secret getaway she scurried out bent low and hurried back to the field.

The Old Shop

She busied herself collecting the items JP had said he needed for the potion. It wasn't long before she had collected everything and was heading back towards the shop.

Two doors away from the shop stood two women in flowery dresses and aprons talking animatedly and pointing towards the shop doorway.

It felt like time had stood still as Amy watched from behind a small tree on the edge of the field. The women talked and talked and talked, would they never stop, she thought, this was wasting time.

On and on they gossiped until eventually they disappeared back into their cottages.

Amy scurried back over the road, the bottle of open sesame potion already in her hand. One drop on the lock and she was quickly back inside the murky shop.

As Amy entered the cellar she found JP filling a blue water pistol with some liquid from a rusty tin.

"What's that?" Amy asked as she placed her ingredients on the floor.

"It's a quick potion I made while you were out. I call it Magical Magnetism. If you squirt some of it onto someone they turn into a human magnet and attract metal objects which stick to them like glue. I thought it might help."

"Do you have a potion in the other water pistol?"

"Yeah, that one's called Blind Storm. It might come in useful too."

And I thought he was walking around with a toy gun filled with water. She felt a little ashamed, maybe there was more to this boy than met the eye, even if he was a little arrogant and too bossy. Before Amy could ask him what the Blind Storm potion did he pointed at the overturned table.

"Can you help me with that?"

They pulled the table over to the corner where there was a small fire burning in the hearth, then they took the items Amy had collected from the field and placed them on the floor behind the table.

Amy Alice and the Alchemists

"Will we have the right stuff?" Amy asked as she rummaged through a pile of medicine bottles JP had scavenged from the cellar and the shop.

"Yes there are plenty of roots which are the main ingredients in a hiding potion like Calmer Chameleon, and I always carry a few essentials in my pockets for emergencies." he looked at Amy before adding in his poshest, most embarrassing voice ever, "All good Alchemists should always be prepared for any eventuality."

Amy cringed, just get on with it she thought, we haven't got time to mess about.

A large tin was filled with pond water and hung over the fire.

"Hairs from the root of the Bullbush plant," JP recited as he sprinkled some course black hairs into the water. "Copper, Mercury and Sulphur in equal measures, mixed together and added at the same time as the first bubble bursts."

JP held a concoction of the three over the tin and waited patiently for the first bubble to appear as the water became hotter. Just as the first small bubble formed on the surface and burst JP poured the mixture into the water.

Amy sat behind the table watching every action silently.

Almost immediately the now yellow water started to boil ferociously.

"Remove from the fire and allow to calm," he lifted the tin off the fire and placed it onto the floor. "add the roots of the Burrowing Ivis and the Creeping Sweetly," he dropped two different types of roots into the can and stirred it, "introduce the camouflage items to the pot. First the stone for hiding in houses, then the grass to hide in fields, leaves for woods and trees and a handful of soil for hills." He hung the tin over the fire once again. "A drop of Silencium, a pinch of Invisitum." these were added with a flourish. "And finally we add a sleeping tonic." From a crusty dark bottle he poured a thick green liquid.

The potion boiled and bubbled in the makeshift cauldron and JP crouched behind the table motioning for Amy to do the same.

"Why are we......." Amy started to ask.

JP put a finger to his lips instructing her to be quiet.

The Old Shop

"It's a hiding potion and it doesn't like to be seen," he whispered.

This is stupid thought Amy, how will it know it's only a liquid.

As the potion bubbled in the tin a small yellow cloud began to form just above the surface. The cloud rolled around inside the tin, it started to circle the interior as if searching for a way out. The cloud climbed the side of the tin and appeared to peer over the rim.

Crouched behind the table Amy had a terrible feeling something was searching for her, sniffing her out, trying to find out where she was hiding.

Swaying from side to side, sensing the air the cloud reached out closer to the table. It stopped moving, leaned closer until it was virtually touching the overturned table, it hesitated, and apparently satisfied sank slowly back into the liquid with a loud pop.

Amy's dark sense of foreboding disappeared as the cloud melted away and JP, apparently feeling the same, peered over the edge of the table. Seeing that the cloud had disappeared he removed the tin from the fire.

"What happens now?" whispered Amy.

"Wait until it cools and put it in the bottle."

As soon as the new Calmer Chameleon potion had been bottled they left the shop and headed back to the farmhouse.

Amy Alice and the Alchemists

The Sewer

Amy and JP lay under the branches of the oak tree on the cold damp soil at the edge of the field, a fine drizzle of rain fell through the early morning sky. They had been here for a while now hidden from sight by the magical camouflage potion JP had made.

The farmhouse remained silent and dark, Amy was itching to get out of this hole in the ground and find out if granddad was alright.

Peering through the drizzle she watched as the door to the farm opened. A large dark figure appeared, he locked the door and lumbered over to the barn which concealed the orange van. As he approached the van Amy strained to catch a glimpse of his face, the collar of the long overcoat was turned up protectively against the rain hiding him from view.

A few seconds later and the van made its way cautiously around the water filled potholes in the dirt track and headed towards the village.

They scrambled from their uncomfortable hideaway and made their way towards the farm house. JP led the way, Amy holding onto the back of his invisible coat. They moved at a snails pace frustrating Amy even more, she wanted to rush right in but the potion wouldn't allow it.

Amy Alice and the Alchemists

It was a long time before they reached the kitchen window, the frame squealed loudly as JP pushed it open and they waited nervously to see if the sound had alerted anyone.

Silence!

They climbed through the open window and made their way to the butcher's room and the trapdoor to the cellar.

Unbeknown to them, leading all the way back to the field, was a long trail of muddy footprints!

Again they paused in the butcher's room, Amy had the same awful sick feeling she had felt earlier when she stood here, she tried to close her eyes, tried hard to ignore the bloodstains on the walls and floor. They carefully lifted the trapdoor and stepped into the dark hole they had opened up in the floor, JP slowly lowered the trapdoor back into place. As he closed the door the light was extinguished from the cellar and they stood on the steps waiting for their eyes to become accustomed to the dark, cold space.

They tiptoed quietly down the stone stairs. The cellar had a low ceiling and every inch of the bare stone walls appeared to be covered by cobwebs. They stood at the bottom of the stairs and faced a locked door. It was obvious that the door was locked due to the amount of chains and padlocks which crisscrossed its surface. Whatever was behind the door was not meant to be found!

JP took the open sesame potion and poured a couple of drops onto each padlock. The tiny silver caterpillars crawled everywhere, as each locked popped open JP carefully laid it on the floor and made sure the chains hung silently from the wall.

Amy stood in a corner and JP braced himself ready to open the door, they were still well camouflaged and would be invisible to whoever was inside. He pushed the door open and was faced with a long low extension to the cellar dug into the earth. Nearest to them in the cave like room were four dirty unmade beds. The bed frames were made from thin planks of wood that looked like they would fall to bits at any minute. The heavy grey blankets lying untidily on the beds looked coarse and uncomfortable.

The Sewer

Several ever burning lights fastened to the wall at the other end of the room bathed this part in a soft golden glow. In the corner lay a ramshackle pile of discarded garden tools.

Amy and JP moved further into the room towards the light where four figures appeared to be working around a large wooden table, as they moved closer a strong smell seemed to fill the room, a nasty foul smell that was getting stronger and stronger.

This end of the room had been converted into a laboratory, some of the items looked as if they could have been taken from the old shop in the village and Amy wondered whether this was the reason it had been deserted. Whoever had built this laboratory wasn't an Alchemist, the equipment scattered about was modern and shiny too new for traditional methods.

The four grey haired men were old, three of them had beards of varying lengths from a straggly, thick chin covering to a long flowing beard which reached the owners belly. The spectacles that they each wore had shiny silver frames, the frame of one pair had been broken and later repaired clumsily with sellotape. All four wore normal white chemists coats, the coats must have all been the same size as the smaller of the men had a coat which trailed the floor and the largest mans coat was tight across his chest, the sleeves barely passing his elbows.

Amy and JP approached the men, the potion was beginning to wear off and their shimmering outlines began to appear.

As they gradually came into view their movements began to speed up, they were back to normal as they reached the table the men were working at.

"Granddad!" Amy called.

The only one of the chemists without a beard was Bernard Alice, Amy's granddad.

"Granddad, it's me Amy."

No response.

She moved closer until she was stood by his side, and tugged at his sleeve.

"Granddad can you hear me?"

Nothing.

JP was now standing by the little old man with the long grey beard waving his hand in front of the chemists face.

"Master, it's me JP are you alright?"

The old chemist carried on working, a vacant expression on his face. JP examined him closely, his eyes seemed glazed and unfocused, his movements were slow and methodical, as if he wasn't in control, as if he was on auto pilot.

Looking around they realised that all four were exactly the same, all unaware of their presence, all deaf to their calls, each one in his own little world.

"Who are they?" Amy asked nodding towards the other chemists.

"These are the four members of the council of the guild. They are the most senior Alchemists in the country and they have been disappearing regularly for the last couple of years or so, obviously to be kept here as prisoners." He had recovered that same superior tone to his voice which aggravated Amy so much.

"What do you think is wrong with them?"

"I think they are under some sort of mind control." said JP.

"It's as if we weren't here." Amy felt scared, "I don't like this, let's get them out."

She took hold of her granddads arm and tried to pull him towards the door but he pulled away from her grasp and kept on working. They couldn't budge any of them, their efforts to get them to leave were in vain.

"Why do you think they have been brought here?" Amy asked on the verge of tears.

JP looked around the room for clues, a row of potions lined a single shelf on one wall and below it lay a large pile of pots, cans, teapots, pans and mugs all dirty and stained, each one made from metal.

"I'm not sure," he said, "but we need to find out what, or who, is controlling them and try to work out a way to get them to stop."

The Sewer

"That won't be easy," Amy felt out of her depth, totally at a loss as to how she could save the four men before her.

"I'm sure we'll manage it, we got this far didn't we?"

"Wait a minute," something had just occurred to Amy, "we only saw one kidnapper leave, but two definitely brought granddad in here." they glanced around nervously, "Where do you think the other one is hiding?"

"They could be anywhere." JP answered.

As JP moved around the table to be closer to Amy he noticed a small opening in the wall behind her which he hadn't been able to see at first.

"I wonder if that's were they went?" he pointed over Amy's shoulder "I'll check it out."

"I'll go, I'll be better in the dark than you."

"Don't be silly, it could be dangerous. I don't want you getting scared."

Amy realised this was the time when she would have to explain about her special powers.

"I'll be able to do it, I'm not as defenceless as you think!"

"Yeah right," he said in a mocking tone of voice, "I still think I should go. I mean, what good will you be without me to protect you."

That's it she thought, I'm sick of your bossy attitude, It's time you had a little shock.

"When you came in the house do you remember the cat with one white eye?"

"Yes." he said irritably.

"That was me!"

He started to laugh, "Don't be ridiculous, that's impossible."

"You don't believe me? Just watch!"

Amy changed herself back into the same cat. She sat looking at him, her head cocked to one side and a triumphant gleam in her green eyes.

She changed quickly back into herself, overjoyed at the amazed look on JP's face.

Amy Alice and the Alchemists

"Told you so!" as she disappeared into the dark tunnel Amy was giggling to herself. The sound of her footsteps disappeared as her shoes became soft paws silent on the stone floor.

JP was shocked senseless, he couldn't believe what he had just seen. He stood rooted to the spot staring wide eyed and open mouthed as the cat's tail disappeared around the corner.

The Amy-cat padded down the narrow stone steps, the smell she had sensed in the cellar was stronger here and became more and more unbearable the further she descended. Water dripped lazily from the rough stone walls and ceiling, green mould grew thickly and the smell was stronger than ever, as if she was stood in a room full of a thousand of the foulest, dirtiest toilets imaginable.

The deeper she went the damper and darker it became, the light from the cellar above a distant glow far behind her. The stone stairway became narrower only just wide enough for one person to squeeze through. The cat's supple body emerged from the fissure with ease into a high vaulted cavernous tunnel.

To her left the tunnel was sheer blackness, but to her right several Ever Burning lights lit the way along a narrow rocky footpath. The footpath ran along side a fast moving, foul smelling river of grey brown water, the stench from the water told her that she was in a sewer.

The kidnappers must use this footpath, she thought, but why, where did it lead. She set off at a trot following the row of flickering lights.

Several high pitched squeaks alerted Amy to the presence of the residents who lived here. The cat instincts that where zipping around inside her told her to go on the hunt, but the Amy instincts, and fears, took charge and instructed her to get out as quickly as possible.

She ran quickly through the dimly lit sewer aware of the hundreds of piercing eyes glaring at her from the shadows, their shrill, high pitched squeaking ringing in her ears. Amy couldn't think of anything worse than being stuck in a dirty smelly sewer with hundreds of big black rats and it pushed her on to run faster.

The Sewer

The lights seemed to go on forever in front of her, and she sensed the rats becoming braver and getting closer and closer, creeping from the shadows. She was beginning to wish she had let JP search the tunnel when she passed the last lamp hanging on the wall by a staircase.

Amy was out of breath but she didn't hesitate and immediately started her precarious climb. This staircase was wider than the one back at the farm, it wound upwards, the steps wet and crumbling under her soft black paws. The air became fresher and the stench faded away as she climbed. Her cat vision guided her safely up the steps, the soft pads of her feet silent on the cold stone. She climbed and climbed and climbed, until suddenly turning a corner she found a heavy mould covered door.

Amy changed back into herself, trying the door she found that it was locked solid. Where was she? What, and who, was behind the door?

Amy Alice and the Alchemists

Mouse in the Mansion

Amy was back to her normal self, the door in front of her locked solid, she groped around in the darkness looking for some way of opening it. The door didn't have a handle so there must be a secret switch somewhere she thought. Wherever it was it remained a mystery, she tried moving rocks, lifting stones, pushing on walls but nothing worked, the door was still locked solid. Amy sat on the cold stone floor trying to work out how she was going to get through, her hand rested on the floor close to the door, a warm draught brushed against her skin tickling her fingers.

She bent down low searching for the source of the breeze and found a small gap under the door allowing the air to seep through.

"Something small will be able to fit under there." she thought.

She started to shrink, whiskers sprouted from her nose which had become pointed, her ears became large and round and a long pink tail extended out along the floor behind her.

The large grey mouse sat on the floor twitching its nose, Amy realised that it had become suddenly darker, she couldn't see a thing everything was blackness. She scurried around on the stone steps searching for the gap under the door. As she was unable to see where she was going she kept bumping into the walls.

Amy Alice and the Alchemists

Amy changed back into herself, with a sigh of relief she found that the darkness had disappeared and she was back in the dimly lit tunnel.

"Wrong mouse!" she whispered as she rubbed her sore nose. "Hickory Dickory Dock," she recited the rhyme as she again became smaller and smaller. This time she had changed into a small brown mouse (with perfect eyesight).

The mouse squeezed under the door with ease, crawling on her belly through the narrow gap she emerged into a dark dusty cellar. Her keen eyesight picked out rows and rows of what appeared to be bottles. The bottles lay on shelves entirely covering the walls of the cellar.

Amy sniffed the air cautiously, her little pink nose picked out nothing but dust and damp. A stairway led upwards from the centre of the wall opposite. That must be the way they went, she thought.

Searching the rest of the room she realised that the door she had crawled under didn't exist. All that could be seen was a continuation of bottle stacked shelves which lined the walls, a secret door leading to the sewer.

Amy headed for the stairs, she skirted the room hugging the edge of the shelves making sure she had plenty of hiding places should someone appear. As she turned the corner, still sticking close to the wall she stopped. She took a few steps back peering into the dark recess between two bottles lying on the floor.

A warm gust of air blew between the bottles, the Amy-mouse twitched her nose, testing the warm air. She picked up a mixture of familiar scents intermingling with the smell of the dust and damp. Intrigued she crawled through the gap between the bottles her soft body moulding itself to the tiny space. She scrabbled her way through, the smells becoming stronger more familiar, the air becoming warmer.

Eventually she found herself in another cellar like room. This room was lit by two ever burning lights held to the walls by ornate brass brackets. The heat in the room emanated from a large open fire which burned in a stone hearth built up so that it towered over the tiny mouse.

Mouse in the Mansion

The hearth extended out from the wall into the centre of the room, stone posts at each corner supported a roof which acted as a chimney ferrying the smoke away from the fire.

As Amy surveyed the room it became obvious that this was an alchemist's laboratory, a real alchemist's laboratory, not like the makeshift one back at the farmhouse. The bellows which protruded from the dominating fireplace were similar to the ones granddad used.

The bottles, jars and vials which littered the room were decorated with signs and symbols which Amy recognised. Several bottles which Amy guessed were potions lined a long shelf, a large box containing plants, dried leaves, roots and bark stood in the corner. A ragged stuffed crocodile which looked like it had been there for hundreds of years hung from the ceiling, suspended by a thin rope.

Amy searched for an exit, scurrying backwards and forwards along the walls. The flickering light from the torches and the fire cast her hurrying shadow against the smooth walls. She searched and searched for a way out, scurrying round and round the walls of the lab. Unable to find any signs of a door she forced her way back through the gap into the wine cellar.

Why would an Alchemist want another secret lab? Why have one at the farmhouse and one here? She couldn't understand it, it just didn't make sense. If there was a lab then the stairs must lead up into a shop. But how many chemist shops had a well stocked wine cellar, again it didn't make any sense.

She made her way quickly to the foot of the stairs. Peering up the darkened staircase she could see a door at the top, it seemed a long way away. Standing on her hind legs reaching up as high as she could she started to climb the stairs, scrabbling for a purchase with her tiny claws her sharp nails dug into the rough stone. Her back legs were kicking and clawing as she dragged herself up onto the step puffing and panting at the effort.

This will take too long, she thought, if anyone comes when I'm halfway up I'll be seen anyway so I might as well get up there as quickly as I can.

Amy Alice and the Alchemists

Without another thought she changed back to herself, she covered the distance to the top of the stairs in a couple of steps. She changed back into the form of the mouse (just in case someone turned up) and listened carefully at the door.

After several seconds she squeezed under the door into a long hallway. Looking both ways along the passageway she could see an open door leading to a kitchen at one end, a door at the other end stood slightly ajar preventing Amy from seeing where it lead. Half way along the corridor in the opposite wall was yet another door, Amy set off towards it.

As she scurried towards the door she heard footsteps approaching. The sound of the footsteps came from the opposite side of the half open door. Amy ran as fast as she could, the footsteps becoming louder and louder, echoing around the hallway. Amy expected the door to open at any second, the footsteps were right outside the door but she was quite a distance from safety, trapped in the narrow passageway with nowhere to hide. Her heart thumping, her eyes wide with fright she stared at the door as she ran hoping against hope that she would have time to hide before the owner of the footsteps opened the door and caught her.

She put on a burst of speed, her tiny feet a blur as she hurtled towards the door closest to her. The footsteps stopped, a few seconds later the door was pulled open. Amy didn't wait to see who appeared, in a flash she threw herself under the door praying that she hadn't been seen.

As she appeared on the opposite side of the door she reeled away in shock as the gaping mouth of a fox leered at her. The fox's eyes glared at her, its teeth bared ready to bite as it towered over the tiny mouse. Amy backed off quickly, bumping into the wall before seeking refuge behind a table leg. She waited for the fox to pounce, readying herself to escape, searching for somewhere safe. Her heart raced faster and faster, her muscles tense, coiled, ready to explode in a life saving sprint to safety.

The attack didn't come. Amy peered around the table leg watching the fox, waiting for it to pounce.

Mouse in the Mansion

The fox remained still, its glassy eyes staring, its mouth gaping in an eternal grimace. She crept from her hiding place, the footsteps had stopped, all was quiet again.

Amy changed back into herself, she searched the room looking for clues as to who lived in the house. She was now in a large study, a dark leather topped desk and chair stood in front of the window. Books on chemistry, science and hunting lined one shelf. Another shelf contained video tapes of pirate adventures, westerns and old horror movies. On one wall hung a feature which, along with the fox, made Amy feel quite ill. The head of a stag adorned the wall, its regal antlers crowning its brow, its large brown eyes gazing peacefully across the room.

Why would anyone want to sit and look at things like this, she thought looking sadly at the deer. The pictures either side of the stags head depicted scenes of red jacketed horsemen surrounded by packs of hounds.

Another question entered Amy's head, why would an Alchemist who only used plants or minerals in his potions want to hunt and kill animals, she was becoming more and more curious as to who the mysterious owner of the house could be.

Amy left by a door which led from the study into a grand, wood panelled room. Banners showing symbols for elements used in alchemy decorated the walls. The room was filled with large round tables, each one holding a small silver cauldron surrounded by tiny vials of liquid as their centerpieces.

Light filtered into the room through a huge arched window, in front of the window stood a long, ancient looking table and four high, elegant, ornately carved chairs.

The banners, the cauldrons, the throne like chairs. This was an alchemists meeting place Amy guessed, a room used by alchemists to discuss disappearances perhaps? A room like this in a mansion sized house, it couldn't be, could it? It had to be, it was too much of a coincidence. This must be DrakeDale!

Amy Alice and the Alchemists

Amy was by now totally confused, why would an Alchemist, a member of the guild, someone regarded as a friend, kidnap other Alchemists? Why, and more importantly, who would do such a thing? Granddad never did tell Amy who owned the house but it was obvious that they were very rich.

The door which Amy had just entered was flung open, Amy gasped in shock.

"You!" screamed a large blond haired woman staring at Amy in surprise. She had obviously seen the Amy mouse run under the door and wasn't prepared to be confronted by a young girl.

Amy froze, the woman paused. Within a split second Amy had recovered her wits, she disappeared in the blink of an eye to be replaced by the tiny brown mouse.

The woman stormed towards the mouse screaming in anger, stamping her heavy black boots down onto the tiny soft body of the mouse. The mouse darted here and there, zipping out from under the crushing blows of the heavy boots.

The woman screamed and cursed, her face red with rage. The Amy-mouse darted back into the study closely followed by the irate woman. She scurried under the desk trying to hide from her attacker. The woman picked up an armful of books from the shelf and flung them at Amy who crouched in fear, the hurtling literature missing her by millimetres.

The door to the corridor stood open, Amy took her chance. She scurried along the base of the bookcase hurrying as fast as she could as books rained down behind her. She stopped suddenly as a book slammed into the floor just in front of her nose.

Another book caught her tail spurring her into action, she ran as fast as she could, she was almost at the door when a particularly heavy volume of "Hunting Through The Ages" hit the fox. The stuffed animal rocked on its plinth, it teetered on the brink towering precariously over the frozen, petrified mouse.

Mouse in the Mansion

As the fox slammed onto the floor Amy tried to dart for safety, she lunged for the doorway but was stuck fast, caught by the tail.

The weight of the inanimate carnivore held the struggling mouse in a vice like grip. The woman stormed towards the trapped mouse, her big fat hands closing in on the wriggling rodent.

Amy, fearing the worst, realised her only chance of escape was to change into something else. As the woman grabbed towards her she changed into a scrawny looking hare. The hare sped off out of reach of the grasping hands, a tiny piece of its fluffy white tail poking out from under the fox.

As the Amy-hare bounded down the corridor with the sounds of angry screaming coming from the study she felt quite tired. She was just about to lie down for a little nap when a flying book whizzed past her bringing her to her senses and she changed again. While still hopping along the hallway she sprouted wings, silky black feathers sprouted out all over her body, her ears shrank and her twitching nose was replaced with a shiny yellow beak. The black bird soared up towards the ceiling pieces of pie crust dropping from its plumage. She flew through the open doorway into a large regal entrance hall.

Amy flew up to hide amongst the glittering chandelier which hung from the high ceiling. The ceiling, which was decorated with intricate mouldings and carvings, was supported by three large stone columns creating four archways leading from what was obviously the front door to the wide staircase.

Dotted around the hall were smaller stone pillars each one supporting an expensive looking statue or vase, pictures and tapestries adorned the walls.

The Amy-bird hid amongst the dazzling crystals of the chandelier watching as the woman charged into the hall her head swinging from left to right searching for the hare.

Amy watched carefully as the woman stopped searching, unable to find any signs of the hare, or girl, or mouse, or what ever she had become. The woman appeared to study something in her mind, concentrating for a second deep in thought.

Apparently making her mind up she stomped across the hallway, she climbed the stairs turning right where they split into two smaller staircases before making her way along the landing.

The woman tapped quietly on a door.

"Enter." came a voice from inside.

As the woman entered the room, closing the door behind her, the Amy-bird flew down to find out if she could hear anything, discover exactly what was going on and uncover the mystery of who the kidnapper was.

"Ah, Beth. Is there a problem?" a man's voice, a voice Amy thought she recognised. But it was too quiet, she couldn't hear properly, she must be mistaken.

"I'm afraid there is sir!"

"What is it exactly? Seth hasn't broken something again has he, he is so clumsy. If he wasn't your brother I would have fired him a long time ago."

"No, Seth hasn't done anything." there was a slight tinge of anger in the woman's voice. Amy had the impression that Beth didn't appreciate the remark about her brother.

"Well what is it?"

"It's hard to explain sir. It would be better if I could show you."

"I'm very busy at the moment, can't it wait?"

"I'm afraid not sir, you must come now." she pleaded.

"Very well, but try and make it quick."

As the footsteps neared the door Amy flew back to her hiding place in the chandelier. Beth made her way down the stairs closely followed by a man who Amy knew. She couldn't believe it, she almost fell from her perch with shock.

Samuel!

It couldn't be, granddad had said they didn't get on, but kidnapping him was taking things a bit far. The traitor, how could he, and why would he do it? Anger like she had never experienced surged through Amy at the thought of what Samuel had done. She had to fight to control the urge to swoop down onto the perfectly groomed head of her great uncle.

Mouse in the Mansion

They crossed the hallway and back into the corridor. Amy fluttered down to the floor watching as the two figures disappeared down the stairs towards the cellar. He was probably off to the farmhouse to gloat at his poor captives she thought angrily as she hopped towards the cellar entrance.

Amy Alice and the Alchemists

Doppelgangers Delight Revisited

Amy had changed back into a cat as she followed the treacherous pair. The rats living in the sewer were becoming braver as she slowly made her way along the smelly tunnel, they crept closer and closer and she had to hiss and spit several times to frighten them off. Their beady eyes shone in the dark piercing into her and the sight of their scaly pink tails disappearing into the shadows made her shiver with revulsion. She hurried after Beth and her uncle keen to escape from this horrid place.

The Amy-cat sat on the dark staircase around the corner from the lab hidden out of sight. In the laboratory Beth was talking to Samuel.

"Now you can see what I have been doing," she said.

"I don't understand, I only asked you to find me a new potion so I could be promoted to Master Alchemist and match my brother's achievements. I never dreamed that you would resort to kidnapping people." Samuel sounded disgusted, Amy realised that the concern he was expressing was genuine. He hadn't been aware of what was going on at all.

Amy Alice and the Alchemists

"When you first asked Seth and I to steal potions for you that was what we did. But then we realised what Alchemists were trying to discover. The secret of turning ordinary metal objects into gold was a much more tempting desire than your petty jealousy." she started to sneer as she spoke giving Amy the impression that she was enjoying herself.

"Turning things into gold. Is that what this is all about? You want to get rich." he started to laugh. "The last Alchemist to discover the secret died over 400 years ago."

"Stop it!" she screamed, "I have gathered the greatest chemical minds in the country. They will discover the secret or they will never leave." ranting manically her madness clear to see.

"Why are you telling me this now after all this time?"

Amy had crept to the very edge of the shadow at the top of the stairs where she could see part of the cellar. Beth was standing with her back to the stairs.

"I'm telling you because it is about time you worked for me. I've slaved after you for years, pandering to your every whim, and for what, the peanuts you call a wage." her voice had grown louder, more aggressive. "I need you to deal with the girl, she's here somewhere I saw her in the house but neither Seth nor I can deal with her and her infernal shape changing. You will do it for me."

"What do you mean shape changing, I don't understand. How will I be able to do it if she's as dangerous as you claim her to be?"

Amy had never thought of herself as dangerous before, her confidence grew as she listened to their argument.

"You will find out soon enough."

"What if I won't do it?" he had become a little nervous, his confidence ebbing away as he was confronted by Beth's anger.

"You will, believe me, you will." threatening him, mocking him, "and when you do you will have the potion I have found for you."

Dopplegangers Delight Revisited

"Potion, what potion?" She had ignited his interest.

"A very special concoction created by your brother here."

"What does it do?"

"It turns you into a shape changer, like I have said the little girl can change into anything she wants."

"I still don't understand what you mean by shape changing." Samuel stepped into view on the far side of the table a confused frown creasing his forehead.

"When we tried to steal the potion she changed into a strange creature, something like a troll or an ogre, and overpowered Seth."

"Changed into a troll." his eyes widened, "That's impossible, where is this potion?"

"I don't know, but I'm going to get a new one from him," she nodded her head at Bernard who was busy mixing something in a large bowl.

"Bernard." the tone of her voice changed becoming smoother, deeper. She talked slowly, her voice remaining level, a constant monotone. From under her jumper she took a blue crystal, holding it out it spun in front of Bernard's staring eyes. "You will make the shape changing potion for me."

Bernard nodded, he stopped what he was doing. Gliding around the makeshift laboratory he began collecting the ingredients he would need for the Doppelgangers Delight.

"How will we know if it works?" Samuel asked, his craving for a new potion overtaking his disgust, and fear, of what Beth and Seth had done.

"We'll use him." Beth pointed over to a cage hidden in the corner. Inside the cage Amy could see a large fat rat, its nose covered in scars, patches of hair missing as if it had been gnawing at the bars trying to escape. The rodent glared at Beth its chisel like teeth stained yellow.

Not another rat Amy thought as a shiver ran down her back, if I never see a rat again it will be too soon. She was still hidden in the shadows, she looked around searching for someway to help granddad and the others. The crystal seemed to hold the key but how could she get it from Beth. Suddenly she realised that there was no sign of JP!

133

Amy Alice and the Alchemists

I knew it, she thought, he's just a coward he must have ran away as soon as he heard Samuel and Beth climbing the stairs. All that bragging about being given the enviable task of finding the Missing Masters and how he was going to use his potions. I knew it was too good to be true.

It didn't take granddad long to create the potion, a bottle stood on the table in front of Samuel its colour constantly changing.

"Fetch the rat." Beth ordered the oldest Alchemist who dutifully obeyed.

A small amount of potion was placed into a saucer and squeezed through a gap in the bars of the cage. The rat sniffed it cautiously, all the while its eyes fixed on Beth. Obviously impressed by the smell of the potion it lapped at it tentatively before sinking its pointy nose into the colourful liquid drinking it down greedily.

Nothing happened, they watched the rat closely, the rat seemed to be even more interested in them. After several minutes of inactivity Beth became angry.

"You've done it wrong!" she screamed throwing a jar at Bernard. The jar, missing him narrowly, smashed against the wall showering glass on the floor.

It took all of Amy's control not to go charging at Beth, but she knew that she would have to be patient and wait for an appropriate moment.

The rat hiccupped.

At the sound from the rodent Beth and Samuel leaned in close to the cage. The rat started to grow, the sleek sewer stained fur turned ginger, its tail became thick and bushy. Its face was now flatter and broader, one of its narrow eyes misted over as if a grey cloud had invaded its eyeball.

"I don't believe it!" gasped Samuel.

Beth grinned.

Crammed into the cage, its face squashed against the metal bars was a large fierce looking cat.

Dopplegangers Delight Revisited

The cat hissed at its captors baring its rotten blackened teeth. At some point in its scurvy life the rat must have come across this cat, the image ingrained into its limited imagination.

"This potion will make me famous." Samuel held up the bottle, his eyes wide.

"And you will make me rich." Samuel turned to find Beth holding out the crystal.

His eyes were drawn immediately to the glittering blue gem.

"You will do as I say." Beth said softly

"I will do as you say." he repeated, his voice sounding far away.

The Amy-cat reacted quickly, she sprang from her hiding place and leapt at the crystal. Beth moved surprisingly fast for such a big woman, she dodged the flying feline, the crystal disappearing safely beneath her clothing. The cat sailed past her, it landed on the table and skidded across its shiny surface her feet splayed wide trying to find a purchase with her sharp claws.

Beth picked up a broom that was leaning against the wall nearby, she thrust the broom at the cat which had slipped off the end of the table and was now hiding beneath it.

"You won't get away this time," she snarled before barking orders at Samuel, "get round there and head her off."

Samuel looked at her as if she was mad. "It's only a cat."

"It's the girl, it must be. Now get round there and catch her."

While they were arguing Amy took her opportunity, she darted from under the table heading for the rickety beds. She cowered beneath one of the spindly bunks, searching for a way to escape. Beth stomped over and with one mighty heave upturned the bed.

Amy scrambled towards the stairs leading back up to the kitchen just as the broom slammed into the floor behind her missing her by inches.

A figure appeared on the stairs, Seth stood there holding a bag of food in each hand a confused frown on his face.

Amy Alice and the Alchemists

"Stop her!" screamed Beth, "It must be the girl, stop her!"

Seth dropped his bags and grabbed the cat roughly by the scruff of the neck.

A faint hissing sound came from somewhere in the room. Seth felt something wet hit his face, he wiped at his cheek while searching the shadowy cellar to see where the liquid had come from looking even more confused than ever as he carried the struggling feline back into the lab.

As he passed the metal objects piled in the corner a silver teapot detached itself from the heap, it flew across the room and stuck to Seth's chest.

"What the....!" he pulled at the teapot but it was stuck fast.

Almost immediately a tin mug flew at him, it was just about to strike his face when he dropped the cat and caught the mug with his hand. Amy scurried away, hiding under the bed she waited to see what would happen next.

"You idiot you let her get away."

"Who.... What..?" his head swung from the mug, to Beth, back to the mug and again back to Beth. "I can't get it off." he said dopily pointing at the mug.

"Never mind that find her."

Unnoticed by everyone in the room the ginger rat-cat crammed into the cage had continued growing. Its face was crushed against the bars of the cage distorting its features, making it even uglier than it already was.

Eventually the flimsy cage could take no more pressure, the door burst open releasing the angry creature. A ginger ball of fury hurtled towards Seth, it landed on top of his head its sharp claws digging into his scalp causing thin rivulets of blood to trickle down his face. Seth screamed, the cat hissed and spat.

The cat leapt from Seth's head as Beth swung the broom at it. The bristly head of the broom connected heavily with the bristly chin of Seth. The large lump of a man fell to the floor with a thud.

Dopplegangers Delight Revisited

The ginger rat-cat, after landing nimbly on its feet, headed swiftly for the sewer disappearing in a flash down the dark stairs.

The Amy-cat tried to rush past Seth in the opposite direction towards the kitchen. The prone, dazed figure of Seth recovered his wits enough to grab the hind leg of the fleeing cat.

In the blink of an eye Amy changed herself into a greasy pink pig. The pig slipped from Seth's grasp to go scuttling up the stairs. Seth jumped to his feet, as he chased after her a saucepan flew through the air fastening itself to his back but he didn't appear to notice.

The pig charged through the deserted farmhouse, it ran through the butcher's room, its feet rattling on the bloodstained floor, through the kitchen and up the stairs.

At the top of the stairs she paused to catch her breath but Seth was right behind her. He lunged forward grabbing at her with his large hairy hands forgetting about the mug which prevented him from grasping the fleeing pig. With a squeal she escaped into the bathroom kicking the door closed behind her with her little pink trotter.

Seth had slipped down a couple of stairs when he grabbed at her but now he slowly crept towards the door, a hideous grin on his battered and bleeding face.

"Little pig, little pig, let me come in." he taunted.

Taking hold of the handle he thrust the door open and stopped in his tracks. A scream started to well up in his throat but he was too terrified to make a sound. Rooted to the spot he gawped wide eyed at the huge wolf which stood grinning at him in the bathroom.

The wolf stood on its fat hind legs, a large, round, pot belly sagged towards the floor. It grinned at Seth, its mouth full of huge sharp teeth.

"Not by the hairs of my chinny chin chin!" it laughed huskily.

The wolf took in a gigantic mouthful of air, its chest expanded monstrously, it raised itself right up onto the tips of its toes and then it blew. It leant forward towards Seth its eyes screwed tight closed, its cheeks puffed out the size of footballs.

Amy Alice and the Alchemists

The air from its lungs hit Seth like a hurricane. The tornado like wind carried him along the landing rolling head over heels, powerless against its ferocity until he crashed painfully into the wall.

Seth scrambled to his feet and charged at the wolf his body crying out in pain, the metal utensils still stuck fast to him.

The wolf took in an even bigger lungful of air forcing it out through its hairy pursed lips. Again Seth was swept off his feet, he tumbled through the air crashing into the wall with a bone crunching thud before slumping to the floor. The impact of Seth hitting the wall had loosened some of the stonework, a large lump of plaster and bricks fell down on top of his unconscious body burying him beneath the dust and rubble.

The Chase

The slow cumbersome footsteps of the wolf echoed around the cellar as it descended the stone stairs. It wasn't a very healthy looking wolf, it looked ill, in fact it looked really bad with its bloodshot eyes and its sagging pot belly swaying to and fro as it walked. The wolf paused at the bottom of the steps, mainly to catch its breath. It watched Beth at the other end of the room as it scratched noisily at one of its hairy armpits. Beth stood glaring back at the wolf the broom held menacingly in her hands.

The wolf approached slowly, snarling in its most aggressive, fiercest way.

"Give me the crystal." it growled.

"Why don't you try and take it." Beth challenged.

The four Alchemists carried on with their work oblivious to what was happening.

Beth and the wolf circled the table, and the men, eyeing each other, looking for weaknesses.

Amy huffed and puffed as she moved, feeling hot and tired she watched Beth carefully. I can't blow her away, she thought, I'll hurt granddad and his friends, I'll just have to fight her to get the crystal but hopefully it won't take long. She sneezed loudly, a shower of wolf snot covered the coat of the nearest alchemist.

Amy Alice and the Alchemists

"Samuel." Beth's voice had again become smooth and intoxicating.
"Kill her."

Amy had forgotten about Samuel, when Beth spoke she noticed him
slumped in the corner apparently asleep.

At the sound of her voice his eyes opened, he climbed groggily to his
feet. His eyes focused on the Amy-wolf, his lips widened in a sly grin. He
held a bottle in one hand, without taking his eyes from the wolf he drank the
remaining mouthful of liquid, hurling the empty bottle away.

Oh, no, thought Amy, that was the Doppelgangers Delight!

As she watched, Samuel began to grow. His chest expanded, ripping
and tearing his shirt, his arms bulged, and his shoulders broadened as he
grew taller and taller. The features of his face changed, eyes reddening, nose
widening and ears lengthening. From his forehead grew two enormous
curved horns each one ending in a razor sharp tip which scraped against the
low ceiling. Samuel ripped away his tattered clothes to reveal that his legs
were now covered in hair, his feet transformed into hooves.

Oh my God, thought Amy as she watched the transformation, what
sort of an imagination does he have to become a creature like this!

What Amy didn't know was that Samuel loved to watch adventure
films with pirates and cowboys, he also liked to watch old horror films. The
creature that he had become, half bull half man, was from one of these scary
films.

Samuel was a Minotaur!

The Minotaur bellowed, the thunderous roar shook the walls of the
cellar. Lowering its head he charged at the Amy-wolf, scattering furniture
and Alchemists, the dagger like horns pointed right at her hairy fat belly.

I'll never be able to beat him like this, she thought, and just as she
was about to be skewered she changed.

The Minotaur thundered past where, a second ago, the wolf had
stood. It charged into the wall, the sharp horns cutting into the stone as if it
were butter. With a mighty heave of its bulging muscles it withdrew itself
from the wall turning to search for its target.

The Chase

Flying out of reach near the ceiling was a tiny golden glow. On closer inspection the glow turned out to be a fairy. A tiny fairy wearing a glittering pink tutu, a small diamond encrusted tiara perched on its head. The fairy hovered in the air, its tiny diaphanous pink wings beating rapidly.

"Kill her!" screamed Beth.

The Minotaur snatched and grabbed at the Amy-fairy who flittered about easily dodging his attempts to catch her.

Beth ran to the other end of the cellar, rummaging through the pile of broken tools she emerged with a small fishing net attached to a long bamboo pole.

As she swung the net at the fairy, a faint hissing sound came from somewhere in the room. She wiped at her cheek which she found was covered in a wet, pungent liquid. Drying her hand on her clothes she again prepared herself, ready to net the little fairy who was dipping and spinning in the air as the Minotaur swung at it clumsily, bellowing with rage.

Beth waited for an opportunity to pounce, but found her vision beginning to fade, as if the room was filling with a thick grey fog. The fog deepened and deepened until, within seconds, she was totally blinded by the thick grey mist. She dropped the net, her arms held out protectively, searching for safety. The now blind woman stumbled around the cellar, a large grey cloud encircled her head. The cloud rolled and tumbled about, every now and then a small lightening bolt would flicker in the cloud followed by a deep rumble.

Beth thought that she was caught in the worst storm ever, she couldn't see a thing and she was deafened by the thunder. She searched for a wall, something to hold onto, her arms waving in front of her, her feet inching forward nervously. Then she fell, she tumbled forward, her arms now waving to protect herself, the ground disappearing under her feet.

Beth was a big woman, she fell heavily down the stairs, her body banged and crashed on the stone steps breaking bones, bruising flesh. She rolled to a stop on the rocky pathway groaning in pain.

Amy Alice and the Alchemists

She sat up rubbing her head, the cloud still covered her face preventing her from seeing where she was but due to the stench it was obvious she had fallen into the sewer. She checked herself for breaks, her ankle, which was now swollen and hot throbbed painfully. Her hand wandered to her chest, more out of habit, to check the crystal. To her horror she found that it was missing. It must have come off during the fall. She rolled over onto her knees scrabbling through the dirt, blindly trying to find her beloved gem.

When the Amy-fairy had seen Beth fall she had zoomed down the stairs after her leaving the irate Minotaur stranded at the top of the narrow opening.

The fairy now watched as Beth searched on hands and knees, sobbing pathetically.

"Where are you?" she cried, "come to momma, your mine, you can't leave me."

The fairy landed on the floor behind Beth, she grew bigger, she stood on four legs, a long straggly beard dangled from her chin, two thick gnarled horns sat curled on her head.

The big black Billy goat pawed at the ground, it took a couple of steps backwards, reared up onto its hind legs and then charged at the great wobbling bottom of Beth. The goats horns crashed into Beth, she screamed in pain as she was flung forward headfirst into the dirty stinking water of the sewer.

Beth splashed about in the water still blinded by the cloud, she grabbed for a purchase on the stony walkway but the current was too strong. The swift flowing river pulled her away from the edge into the deeper water, whisking her away into the dark tunnels of the sewer where only the rats dared to go. The last thing Amy saw was her outstretched hand slowly sinking below the choppy brown surface.

Amy's concentration was broken by a blood curdling howl from the top of the stairs. She looked up to see a wiry, grey, mad looking werewolf.

The Chase

The werewolf had the same red eyes as the Minotaur but it was a lot smaller, Samuel had obviously changed to be able to fit through the stairs. Its long, black tongue hung from its mouth, drool dripping in lazy droplets from its chin. The werewolf bounded down the stairs howling in fury as it came.

There was nothing else to do but run, and Amy ran for her life. Her hooves clattered on the stone floor as she galloped along the dark path, the torchlight flickering lazily. The werewolf was too fast, it was gaining on her rapidly. Amy could hear it close behind her, its insane howling and snarling echoing around the cavernous tunnel, ringing in her ears. As the creature closed in it lunged at her, its spindly clawed hands reaching out ready to tear into her. Amy kicked out with her sharp hooves catching the werewolf in the ribs. The monster was forced back growling and snapping at her. This gave Amy the split second she needed to escape, she changed back into the fairy and sped off away from the sickening monstrosity. The creature howled with rage, charging at her again lashing out wildly but the speeding fairy was far out of reach.

She was almost at the stairway leading to the mansion when she realised the howling had stopped.

The Amy-fairy glanced over her shoulder just in time to see a large black bat closing in on her, its mouth wide open ready to bite down with its needle like teeth.

Amy dropped like a stone, the vampire bat whizzing past her missing her by a whisker. The bat turned quickly, it came storming back at her as she sprinted off, flapping its leathery wings it chased her at high speed.

The speeding doppelgangers ducked and dived in a terrible dance of death, swooping down inches above the choppy stinking water before zooming up towards the crumbling, arched roof. Narrowly evading a charge from above, Amy hurtled up the stairs towards the mansion.

She found the door still open as they had left it; speeding through the wine cellar she flew up the staircase and headed for the hallway, the bat close behind her all the way.

Amy Alice and the Alchemists

Round and round the stone pillars they went, the bat inches from her, closing in all the time. In and out of the ornate vases they sped before rising up to orbit the chandelier, the fairies golden glow reflected in the crystals, dappling the room with twinkling starlight. Amy danced in the air, dropping down, rising up, twisting and turning in a desperate effort to escape from the bat, but to no avail.

She was beginning to tire, her wings ached, her lungs screamed for air, but still the bat came after her tirelessly. The bat chased her round one of the pillars which supported the domed ceiling, climbing as they went, like a corkscrew rising up towards the ceiling. The bat flew around the pillar, its mouth open in a hideous, deathly grin, ready to sink its teeth into the delicate body of the fairy.

As it closed in, the fairy put on a final burst of speed, she disappeared out of sight around the pillar. Not to be outdone, the bat flapped its wings furiously, trying to close down on the fairy. As it turned the corner it realised that it had been tricked, the bat panicked, for the first time it felt afraid.

The Samuel-bat screeched to a halt, its wings desperately trying to change its direction as it hurtled in towards the gaping mouth of the largest rat it had ever seen. The rat clung to the stone pillar with its sharp claws, its thick scaly tail lashing excitedly from side to side. On its head it wore a golden crown, a purple, ermine trimmed cloak covered its back.

The momentum of the bat carried it into the rats reach, the rodent clamped down on the bats leathery wing with its chisel like teeth. The bat struggled against its captor, lashing its wings against the rats head, squeaking and squealing in pain. The rat held on tight, driving its sharp teeth through the bats wing, piercing the thin membrane.

Then the bat was gone, the rat found itself biting down on the large red feather of a brightly coloured parrot. The parrot took its chance, beating its wings it soared away from the gnashing teeth of the rat. Looking back at the rat the parrot didn't notice the fishing net come sailing through the air until it was too late and he was dragged to the floor.

The Chase

Unseen hands pinned the surprised bird to the floor, someone forced open its beak pouring a foul tasting liquid down its throat from a bottle that had appeared from nowhere. The squawking parrot coughed and spluttered at the horrid substance it had been forced to take, its one large eye glaring threateningly, searching for its invisible captor.

Samuel wanted to change from the parrot into something more dangerous, something to terrify this unseen assailant. He tried and tried, all the foulest, nastiest creatures he had ever imagined flashed through his head but to no avail. He couldn't change, he remained as he was, a large red parrot with one wooden leg and a black patch over one eye.

"Pieces of eight, pieces of eight." he squawked as he struggled against whoever it was that held him down until, finally, he tired and lay quietly.

The Amy rat scuttled headfirst down the column, it landed softly on the floor changing back into Amy as she approached the parrot.

"JP is that you?" she asked hopefully.

"Yeah, it's me."

"Am I pleased to see you," she squinted hard trying to make out where he was, "well I would be if I could see you. Anyway I'm glad you're here, thanks."

JP began to appear, slowly at first but then more rapidly until she could see him crouched down, his hands still pinning the parrot to the floor.

"What was that potion you gave him?"

"I watched Master Alice make the shape changing potion and I thought that I could make an antidote. So while you were away searching the mansion earlier I got to work."

"You mean he'll always be a parrot?"

"I don't know. He hasn't changed yet so maybe it has worked. What shall we do with him?"

"Take him with us, we'll have to go and get granddad and the others."

Amy Alice and the Alchemists

They headed back through the sewer, obviously nervous from the earlier commotion the rats kept their distance which pleased Amy. As she climbed the stairs towards the farmhouse cellar Amy noticed something glinting in the shadows. Reaching down she found the crystal, its golden chain had snapped during Beth's fall and it had lain here undiscovered.

Back in the cellar laboratory the four alchemists were still busy mixing potions.

"What should we do?" asked Amy, "How can we get them to snap out of it?"

"Destroy the crystal." JP said as he locked the Samuel-parrot into the cage which had earlier held the rat-cat. "It must still be controlling them even though the woman's gone."

Amy placed the crystal on the floor, she picked up a large stone that had been dislodged from the wall by the Minotaur. Pounding the rock down onto the beautiful blue gem with all her strength she shattered it into millions of glittering pieces.

Immediately the four old men stopped working, they stood gazing at each other, each one with a puzzled look on his bearded face.

Question after question was hurled at Amy and JP. It took a long time before the alchemists were satisfied enough to follow them out of the farmhouse and back towards the village to get help.

A New Apprentice

The great hall was crammed with Alchemists all talking excitedly, the four ornate chairs at the long table in front of the arched window still stood empty. The excited alchemists muttered amongst themselves questioning why they had been gathered. What could be so important?

The room fell silent as the large double doors slowly swung open. The four master alchemists entered the room to a standing ovation, they paused at the doorway and smiled at their friends who had burst into sound. The room was filled with the sounds of good wishes, they called out their congratulations, well done's and good to see you back's with great gusto.

The four grey haired alchemists made their way down the centre aisle slowly, the golden trim of their robes and their golden under robes shone brightly as they passed, nodding and smiling at their well wishers.

Being the most senior alchemist of the guild, Albert Ecclestone led the way. He was followed by his three colleagues, each one carrying one of the essentials.

Amy Alice and the Alchemists

Ernest Wellbright, who had been the first to disappear, strode up the aisle carrying a small box containing salt. He had become quite fond of his long flowing beard, he wore it now combed and trimmed with a shining gold ribbon tied to the end. The next one to enter was Duncan Heatherbridge carrying a small ceramic vial containing Sulphur. Duncan's spectacles had been repaired, they glinted in the light of the room but not as bright as the smile which lit up his face like a beacon. The last to reach the table was Bernard, carrying a silver bottle which he placed on the table by the box and the vial before taking his place to stand by his chair.

Albert motioned for the audience to sit, they slowly quietened before taking their seats, their excitement overcoming their normally well observed protocol. Once everyone in the room had sat down, three of the golden robed alchemists also sat to leave Albert stood alone.

"My dear friends, we are overwhelmed by your reception, it is most pleasing and heart warming that you greet us in this manner. As spokesperson of this council it is my duty to make a few announcements."

Several senior alchemists in their purple robes started muttering to each other excitedly. Albert waited patiently, savouring the moment before continuing.

"Firstly, I am sad to say, Senior Alchemist Samuel Alice has decided to retire from the guild."

When they heard this everyone in the room started talking. Questions were fired at Bernard who simply smiled holding out his hands, motioning for silence.

Bernard spoke to Albert in a hushed whisper. "Master Ecclestone, may I be allowed to speak?"

"Certainly." Albert sat in his large chair as Bernard stood to address the concerned faces before him.

A New Apprentice

"My brother sends his regrets that he was not able to inform you personally, and he has asked me to tell you that his decision was hard to swallow. But he has taken an opportunity that was too good to miss, a life changing opportunity. Sadly this means that he won't be back ever again." a cloud of sadness covered his face before brightening as he continued.

"One thing which he has left for us is this house. Samuel has donated the house to the guild to be used whenever we require it."

A spontaneous round of applause echoed around the panelled walls.

"Gentlemen, as you are aware it has been a dangerous, frightening time for us as one by one our friends were disappearing, abducted by an unknown, evil force. However, without the bravery and ingenuity of two young people we may never have defeated these callous greedy creatures. Gentlemen I present to you Apprentice Alchemist of the grey order Jonathan Polldown and my granddaughter Amy Alice."

Bernard pointed towards the doors before taking his seat, all heads turned to face the two young heroes marching down the aisle, their cheeks flushed with embarrassment, huge beaming smiles on their faces. They were both dressed in plain white robes which trailed the floor. They stopped in front of the table bowing their heads in a mark of respect for the council.

"Gentlemen," Albert spoke over their heads addressing the robed congregation, "It has been decided by the council that in recognition of their bravery these two young people shall be rewarded. Jonathan Polldown is now promoted to First Degree Alchemist of the Red Order."

Bernard handed him a red silk sash which had been lying stretched out on the table. JP took the sash, after placing it around his neck he bowed low to Albert.

"Amy Alice has hereby been ordained as Apprentice Alchemist of the Grey Order, the first girl to be so honoured for over a hundred years." Albert called out over the cheering which had already broken out amongst the guild members.

Amy Alice and the Alchemists

He picked up a grey sash and handed it to Amy who placed it tentatively around her neck. With a beaming smile she bowed low before standing by JP.

"Gentlemen I give you JP and Amy Alice!"

They turned to face the crowd who jumped to their feet clapping and cheering madly at the sight of the two new alchemists stood before the four golden robed masters.

Several of them began hurriedly mixing potions in the small silver cauldrons which sat in the centre of each table. Tiny gold stars shot from the shiny pots, they zoomed around the room leaving a glittering trail behind them before exploding in a golden shower to rain down on the cheering crowd below.

Amy and JP grinned widely as their hands were shook till they thought they would drop off and their backs were slapped till they ached. Even Unwin appeared from the crowd to offer his congratulations, his normally sour expression had given way to a beaming smile, his grey hair covered with shiny golden star dust.

Back in granddads flat Amy stood with her nose pressed against the window pane glancing up and down the street.

"When will they be here?" she moaned.

"Soon, soon." he soothed, "come and sit down and relax. They'll be here when they're here, staring out of the window won't make them get home any quicker."

Amy slumped into a chair sulkily, in the corner stood a large shiny birdcage. The Samuel-parrot sat perched inside, his one good eye glaring at Bernard.

"You know, I've been thinking," he said watching the big red bird, "it's quite ironic isn't it, that he's a parrot."

"Why's that?" Amy asked, her head swivelling towards the window at the sound of a passing car.

A New Apprentice

"Well, he's been copying me all my life. Taking from me, using my ideas and now all he can do is mimic what I say."

"Yes I see what you mean." she said slumping further into her chair when she realised the car had driven straight past the shop.

"Pretty boy." Bernard called to the parrot.

The parrot glared at him, fighting the urge to respond but it was no good, its instincts took over making it squawk out loudly.

"Pretty boy, pretty boy!" obviously disgusted with itself it hobbled across the floor of its cage its wooden leg tapping loudly on the metal floor.

The parrot started to eat a sunflower seed, its great hooked beak and thick purple tongue making short work of the hard stripy shell of the seed.

The door to the shop downstairs opened and slammed shut, footsteps could be heard approaching up the stairs.

"It's them!" cried Amy excitedly.

Amy's parents burst into the room, they both wore a T-shirt with a photo of a rhino's face above a caption which read, "I did it for Elizabeth!"

"Mum, dad!" she screamed as she flung herself at them hugging them tightly. "I've missed you."

"We've missed you too." said her dad.

"Has she been good?" mum asked Bernard.

"She's been a big help. I couldn't have gotten through the last few weeks without her!" he smiled.

"Oh, you've got a new parrot!" cried dad.

They crowded around the cage cooing and clucking at the angry looking bird.

"What's he called?" mum asked as she blew big soppy kisses at the parrot.

"We've named him Uncle Sammy." said granddad, "and even though he hasn't been here long, he already feels like one of the family!" he gave Amy a knowing wink.

Granddad looked at Amy his bright eyes gleaming behind the silver rims of his glasses.

"Our secret." he whispered.